SHATTERED

ERIC WALTERS, a former elementary-school teacher, has written over forty bestselling novels and has won numerous awards. He has received honours from the Canadian Library Association Book Awards and won UNESCO's international award for Literature in Service of Tolerance. He lives in Mississauga, Ontario.

LIEUTENANT GENERAL THE HONOURABLE ROMÉO DALLAIRE (RETIRED) was a professional Canadian soldier, serving as commander of the army and later as assistant deputy minister (Human Resources, Military). In 1993, he was appointed commander of the United Nations Observer Mission—Uganda and Rwanda (UNOMUR) and the United Nations Assistance Mission for Rwanda (UNAMIR). His personal account of the 1994 Rwandan genocide, *Shake Hands with the Devil: The Failure of Humanity in Rwanda*, was published to critical acclaim and has become an international bestseller. He was summoned to the Canadian senate in March 2005. He also continues his role as a special adviser to the Canadian government on war-affected children and on the prohibition of small-arms distribution.

Also by Eric Walters from Penguin Canada

The Bully Boys
The Hydrofoil Mystery
Trapped in Ice
Camp X
Royal Ransom
Run
Camp 30
Elixir
Camp X: Fool's Gold

Other books by Eric Walters

Triple Threat
The True Story of Santa Claus
Grind
Overdrive
I've Got an Idea
Underdog
Death by Exposure
Road Trip
Tiger Town
Northern Exposures
Long Shot
Ricky
Tiger in Trouble
Hoop Crazy
Rebound
Full Court Press
Caged Eagles
The Money Pit Mystery
Three-on-Three
Visions
Tiger by the Tail
War of the Eagles
Stranded
Diamonds in the Rough
STARS
Stand Your Ground

SHATTERED

ERIC WALTERS

WITH A FOREWORD BY ROMÉO DALLAIRE

PUFFIN
CANADA

PUFFIN CANADA

Published by the Penguin Group

Penguin Group (Canada), 90 Eglinton Avenue East, Suite 700, Toronto, Ontario, Canada M4P 2Y3
(a division of Pearson Canada Inc.)

Penguin Group (USA) Inc., 375 Hudson Street, New York, New York 10014, U.S.A.
Penguin Books Ltd, 80 Strand, London WC2R 0RL, England
Penguin Ireland, 25 St Stephen's Green, Dublin 2, Ireland (a division of Penguin Books Ltd)
Penguin Group (Australia), 250 Camberwell Road, Camberwell, Victoria 3124, Australia
(a division of Pearson Australia Group Pty Ltd)
Penguin Books India Pvt Ltd, 11 Community Centre, Panchsheel Park, New Delhi – 110 017, India
Penguin Group (NZ), cnr Airborne and Rosedale Roads, Albany, Auckland 1310, New Zealand
(a division of Pearson New Zealand Ltd)
Penguin Books (South Africa) (Pty) Ltd, 24 Sturdee Avenue, Rosebank, Johannesburg 2196, South Africa

Penguin Books Ltd, Registered Offices: 80 Strand, London WC2R 0RL, England

First published in a Viking Canada hardcover by Penguin Group (Canada),
a division of Pearson Canada Inc., 2006
Published in this edition, 2006

1 2 3 4 5 6 7 8 9 10 (OPM)

Author representation: Westwood Creative Artists
94 Harbord Street, Toronto, Ontario M5S 1G6

A percentage of the author's royalties will be donated to charities of benefit to children in Rwanda.

Manufactured in the U.S.A.

LIBRARY AND ARCHIVES CANADA CATALOGUING IN PUBLICATION

Walters, Eric, 1957–
Shattered / Eric Walters ; with a foreword by Roméo Dallaire.

ISBN-13: 978-0-14-331226-0
ISBN-10: 0-14-331226-X

1. Genocide—Rwanda—Juvenile fiction. 2. Peacekeeping forces—Rwanda—Juvenile fiction.
3. Rwanda—History—Civil War, 1994—Atrocities—Juvenile fiction. I. Title.

PS8595.A598S53 2006 jC813'.54 C2006-906566-7

One death is a tragedy; a million is a statistic.

—JOSEPH STALIN

All that is required for evil to prevail is for good men to do nothing.

—EDMUND BURKE

Foreword

I SERVED IN THE CANADIAN MILITARY, as did my father before me. My father was a role model for me, perhaps a bit more stern than I would have liked, but nevertheless a man of high moral standards and example. Much of my success in life is due in no small measure to the values and principles he was able to instill in me. He was my mentor in "ways military," explaining the code of military discipline and the conduct of a non-commissioned officer.

The story you are about to read is not about me, although there are similarities, but it is about a fictional soldier who has been through some of my experiences and many more. He represents a new type of veteran, released from his military family because he can no longer perform his military duties as a result of an injury sustained in operations. Had he suffered a physical injury, he would be accepted in society as an honourable veteran wounded in a foreign war, but this fellow has no visible injuries, so he is seen, as so many others like him, as just another failed soldier, gotten rid of because he is now damaged goods.

It is a case that unfortunately is far too close to reality. The author has captured the frustration of the injured soldier and society's indifference to both him and the street people with whom he lives. In our rush to material success and its rewards, we are prone to stereotype people without pausing to consider the circumstances of the less fortunate and how we can help those who have become marginalized to find some semblance of a tolerable if not a rewarding life.

The worse offence is to fail to recognize these injured people as fellow humans in our wonderfully affluent society. To belittle their condition is unpardonable. We will be looked upon by history by the way we treated our wounded and downtrodden.

In this story, the reader will encounter characters who, over time, discover their own compassion toward those who are wounded. They may well be the heroes of our time.

Roméo Dallaire
Ottawa, October 2005

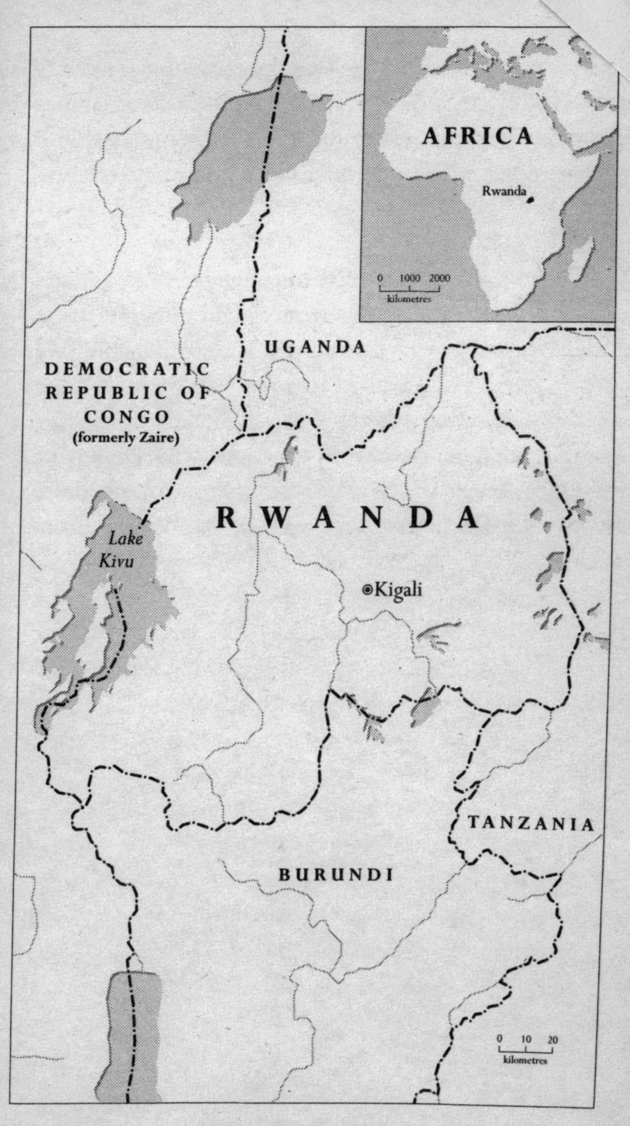

Map of Rwanda

One

I TURNED THE COLLAR UP on my ski jacket. The wind was bitterly cold and was blowing directly into my face. It was the first day of spring but it didn't feel like it. Instead it was just another cold day in an endless winter of cold, snowy days. At least it wasn't snowing right now. It was the coldest winter I could remember. My father told me there was one even worse twelve years ago but I was only three then and couldn't remember that far back.

I looked at my watch. It was almost ten to six. I had just over ten minutes to get there. It wasn't good to be late for a job interview. Then again, it was an interview for a *volunteer* job. What was the worst that could happen? That I wouldn't get a job that didn't *pay* that I didn't *want* to do to begin with?

Then I thought about what would happen if I didn't get the job. My civics teacher had made it clear that if I didn't get this job she wasn't arranging another interview for me. And she'd made it equally clear that if I didn't get a placement, I couldn't pass, and my father had already told me what would happen then. If I didn't get all of my credits there wasn't going to be any car for a birthday present.

My father had promised me a car when I turned sixteen. That was what his father had done for him and what he'd said he was going to do for me. I didn't know what type, but he'd been hinting around about a BMW. It probably wouldn't be anything fancy—maybe something in the 300 series. My father could afford to buy me a Beamer. He could afford to buy a *dozen* Beamers. Maybe he wasn't around that much but the money helped make up for that. Now, thinking about the car, the job interview had some real meaning. I doubled my pace.

As I walked I kept my head up, looking around. I didn't know the downtown very well at all. The times I'd come here were with my parents for hockey games, shows, or shopping and this certainly wasn't the part we'd been to. There were no theatres or fancy stores anywhere to be seen.

Instead the buildings were run-down and seemed to be limited to dollar stores, pawn shops, laundromats, and cheque cashing stores. A couple of the stores had boards over the glass, the boards plastered with posters and advertisements. Some of them even had curtains in the windows—failed retail had become street-level apartments.

The streets themselves were dirty and strewn with garbage. It was dreary and depressing. But that shouldn't have been any surprise to me. Where else would they put a soup kitchen to feed street people?

I shook my head. I still couldn't believe this. I was going to be doing my community hours at a soup kitchen. That sounded like something out of bad movie or a book by John Steinbeck. But I didn't have anybody to blame but myself. Why had I been so stupid? I hadn't bothered to read the information in the booklet listing all the volunteer jobs. I just saw the name of the program—"The Club." I thought it sounded classy. I guess it did have class ... the class possible. Then when my teacher told me what it really was, I couldn't back out. She'd already been on my case about how I was always taking the easiest route, how I always cut corners on assignments, and that I didn't take her class seriously. She was right. I didn't take her class—or any class—seriously. She then went on to tell me how *surprised* she was by my choice and that maybe she'd *misjudged* me. The truth was that she hadn't misjudged me.

She actually made me a little uneasy. I got the feeling that she was always trying to figure everybody out. I hated people like that. Especially those people who actually *did* have you figured out.

I just wished I'd been smart enough to start my placement—any placement—when everybody else had started theirs. Somehow I'd just hoped that I could skate by without doing it. And when she didn't mention it to me, week after week, I thought that somehow she'd forgotten about it too. Now I only had three months to finish up what had taken other people six or seven months to do.

So here I was, heading to the Club. Obviously somebody's idea of a joke. Unfortunately the joke was now on me.

The time was tight. It was still one block down and one block over. There was a park on my right side. If I went through the park I could cut the angle and maybe I could just make it. I turned onto the gravel path that led diagonally across the park—exactly the direction I needed to go.

I'd travelled no more than a dozen steps when I had second thoughts. This wasn't the best neighbourhood and t was starting to get dark. I looked around anxiously. I didn't see anybody. I guess even bums had better places to be than hanging around a park in the cold and dark. I'd keep my head up and my eyes open and—

"You got a smoke to spare?"

I jumped into the air, spun around, and stifled the urge to scream. There was a man standing in the shadows, just off from the path. I'd walked right by him and hadn't seen him at all. So much for keeping my eyes open.

The man stepped out of the shadows and into the open. My heart was still pounding but I took a good look at him. He was dressed in a large, dirty, green parka. He had a matching green toque pulled low on his head, a few days' growth of greying, gritty beard on his face.

"I didn't mean to scare you," he said apologetically. He sounded like he meant it.

"You didn't scare me … I was just … just startled … that's all," I stammered.

"Didn't mean to do that either. You got an extra smoke I can have?"

"I don't smoke."

"Smart. Wish I didn't either. Any spare change?" he asked.

"Sure." I unzipped my jacket and reached inside, pulling my wallet out of the pocket. I opened it up and—

"Put that away!" he snapped.

I looked up at him confused and a little scared. What was he talking about, what did he mean?

"Put that wallet back in your pocket," he ordered.

"But I was just trying to give you some change," I tried to explain.

"I understand that—I appreciate that—but you can waving a wallet around here. You never know who's watching." He looked stern and serious.

Slowly I looked around. There were trees and bushes casting long shadows, but the park was deserted except for him and me. "I don't see anybody."

"Just because you can't see *them,* doesn't mean they can't see *you.*" He paused. "Just put it away."

I stuffed my wallet back into my pocket.

"You just have to be careful," he said. "You never know who's around."

I nodded my head. Did he really think we were being watched or was he just crazy? I'd heard about people like this—what was the word—paranoid, that was it, paranoid. I knew that a lot of the people who lived on the street were mentally ill—psychiatric patients—and that they heard voices in their heads, or saw things that weren't there or believed people were watching them, were out to get them. But this guy didn't seem crazy. Then again, how did I know what was going on inside his brain? If he really was normal, would he be out here begging for change?

"There are people who would split your head open for a couple of bucks and you have more than a couple of bucks—I saw the bills when you opened your wallet."

I stepped back a half step.

"It's not me you have to worry about," he continued. "There's not enough money in any wallet to make me hurt another human being."

I didn't know him—he was just some street person begging smokes and change—but somehow I believed him.

"I think I have some change in my pocket … not much, but some," I said.

"Anything you have would be appreciated," he said softly, looking down at the ground.

I dug into my pocket and rummaged around. There were a few coins jingling together. I pulled them out and looked. There wasn't much—a quarter, a couple of dimes, and three or four pennies. I dropped them into his outstretched hand.

"Thank you," he said.

"You're welcome. I'm sorry there isn't more."

"I appreciate what you gave. Some people, they don't even turn their heads—they act like you're not there." He paused. "It's getting dark," he said. "You shouldn't be here when it's dark."

"I'm just cutting through. I have an interview in—" I looked down at my watch. "Right now. I got to get going." I rushed off down the path.

"Thanks!" he yelled and I looked over my shoulder. He gave a little wave. "Be careful!" he called out. I nodded and kept going.

Strange. Not what I'd expected. A bum who was polite—and well spoken. He had a trace of some sort of accent … I couldn't tell what, but something. There was also something else about him. Maybe it was the manners—I hadn't expected that—or the way he stood. His shoulders were back, his posture perfect. Strange.

With his warning to be careful, I tried to be more aware of what was around me. Coming up to a bench beside the path, I realized that it was occupied. There was a man stretched out on it. He was covered by a tattered old

had to

ahead, coming directly toward me along the path, was a woman pushing a shopping cart. The wheels were digging into the gravel and she was struggling to keep it moving. She was all stooped over and had a pronounced limp. Her clothing was a crazy patchwork quilt of colours and materials and items. The cart was piled high and as she got closer I could see that it wasn't filled with groceries. There were empty bottles, folded cardboard boxes, newspapers, and clothing—rags. She was pushing a cart filled with garbage.

As she got even closer I heard her talking to herself. It was a loud, profane rant about the government. I squeezed over to the very edge of the path to create as much distance between us as possible. As she got close her monologue got louder and louder.

She looked up at me. "Cold one, ain't it," she said, and flashed me a smile.

"Yeah, cold," I mumbled. Crazy but friendly.

I looked back over my shoulder and watched—and listened—as she continued both her journey and her rant. I couldn't help but wonder what was going on in her head. What demons were driving her? But I didn't have time to even think about that. I had to get going as fast as I—

"Hey!"

I jerked my head to the side. Two men—really, older teenagers—were cutting across the grass toward me. I

"Wa

There was no doub

Another man appeared on the path directly in fron

"He told you to wait," the third man said.

A shiver went up my spine as I skidded to a stop directly in front of him. He stood there in the middle of the path, blocking my way. The path was narrow at this point, boxed in by hedges on both sides. It was sheltered … and isolated. I looked past him, up the path. There was nobody in sight.

I turned around. The other two were closing in and there was nobody else in sight in that direction either. Even the shopping cart lady had disappeared around the corner. Quickly they closed the space until they were right behind me and I was caught in the middle, trapped. I felt a wave of panic sweep over me. What did they want? Had they seen me pull out my wallet? Were these the people that guy had warned me about, the people who were watching?

They were all dressed in black, leather jackets, thick-soled boots. They looked like thugs, not people living on the street. I felt scared—no, worse than scared. I almost felt sick.

"Nice shoes," one of them said. He was clearly the biggest of the three—not just taller but thicker, more muscular. The other two weren't much bigger than me.

"Um … thanks," I mumbled. They were practically new, top-of-the line Air Jordans. They were a Christmas present from my grandmother.

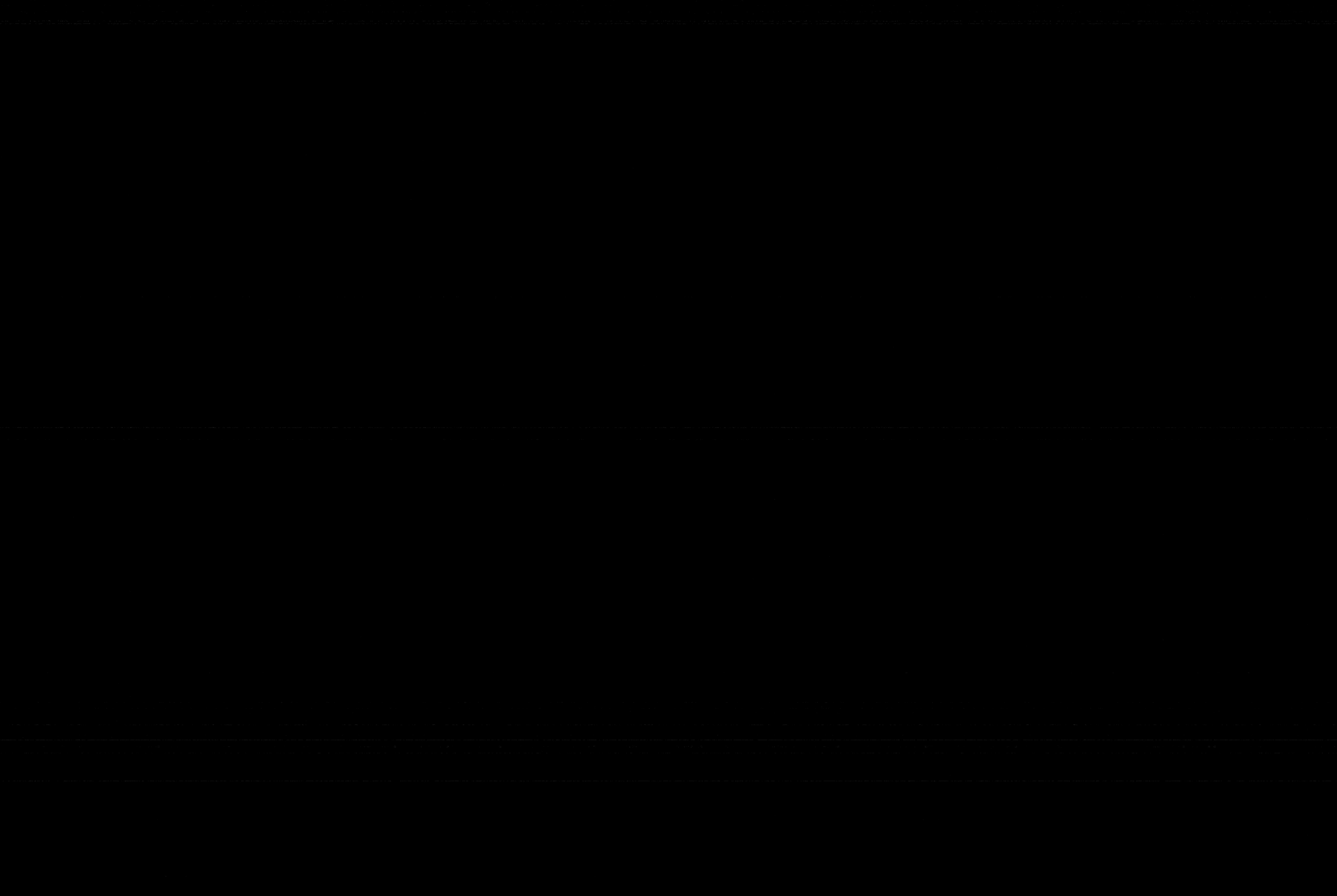

"I'm not lying … honest … I gave away what I had to one of the panhandlers," I explained. My mouth was dry and I could feel my hands trembling, but I still wasn't going to hand over my money to these jerks.

"How nice. You gave some bum your cash and us your shoes. What a nice guy you are," he taunted and the other two began laughing.

"Don't worry about it, man," one of the two behind me said, "the night is still young. We might get that money anyway … if we roll the right bum."

They all started laughing, but there was no joy or happiness in the laughter. It was mean, evil. They weren't just after my shoes or my money. They were enjoying this.

"Now, let's have your coat," the big guy, who was obviously the leader, said.

"Come on, not my coat … please." It wasn't just my coat. It was my wallet in the inside pocket with all of my ID and money. What would they do when they found out I'd lied to them and really did have money?

"Give us your coat!"

"I think he probably wants to keep his coat," came a voice from behind. We all spun around. It was him—the man I'd given the change to.

"If you got half a brain you'd stay out of this," snarled the leader.

"Leave the kid alone," the man said, sounding very calm.

"This ain't your business, you old rubby. Just go away and find yourself some aftershave to drink."

"I'm not leaving without my friend here."

"You stupid or drunk or both?" demanded the guy holding my shoes.

"Just leave the kid alone. He hasn't done anything wrong."

"We'll leave him alone after we get his coat!" the biggest of the three snarled.

"Do you want my coat instead?" the man asked. "You can have it if you want."

"Yours? You think I want to wear something you've worn? Probably filled with lice."

"I don't know about lice, but what about this?" He pulled a long piece of metal out of his sleeve. It was half as long as his arm and as thick as a thumb. The man held the metal rod up, turning it around, like he was examining it for the first time, like he had never seen it before. As it turned, the rod caught some of the fading rays of the sun and glistened.

"Pretty nice, eh?" he asked.

The two guys between us backed away until all three of them stood side by side. I staggered forward so that the man was now between them and me.

"You really think you're scaring us?" the leader asked.

"Not trying to scare anybody. Just want us to walk away in one direction and the three of you go in the other."

"You're not goin' anywhere except down … let's take 'em!" the guy yelled.

The three thugs surged forward. Lightning-like, the man jumped to the side and with his leg swept the feet out from under the leader, who crashed to the gravel with a heavy thud! Almost in the same motion he brought the

toward him,
nd the young guy turned
and ran away. Now [illegible] spun around and leaped forward until he was standing over top of the two thugs.

"Don't move!" he yelled.

I stood stock still before I realized he wasn't talking to me.

One of the two tried to get back up. The man reached over and kicked his arm out from under him and he crashed back down to the ground. The other one was clutching his leg, rolling around in pain.

"Shoes," the man said, pointing the metal rod at them.

"Sure … he can have them … we weren't really goin' to take them," the leader whimpered. He didn't sound so brave now—or look so big. He reached to the ground where my shoes had fallen when he was knocked down. He held them out for me.

Cautiously I inched forward and took them. "Thanks," I said. That sounded stupid.

"Now your shoes," the man said.

"What?" the thug asked.

"I want *all* the shoes. *Your* shoes … and his," he said, pointing at them with the metal bar.

"But—"

"Now!" He took the bar and slammed it against one of the shrubs, causing the wood to splinter.

Both thugs scrambled to undo their laces.

"No, wait!" he ordered. "You get to keep your shoes," he said, pointing to the guy whose leg he'd hurt. He

The thug loo

he was going to say so

took off his second shoe and ... pped out of his jacket.

"Get up."

The injured one had trouble rising—he was barely able to put weight on the one leg. He was grimacing in pain and his face was stained with tears.

"Now get out of this park and I don't ever want to see either of you back here again."

"This isn't the end," the big guy said. Suddenly, on his feet, he was feeling more confident again.

"It is the end unless you want to lose your *pants* as well."

I almost laughed but restrained myself. The thug now seemed more comical than threatening as he stood there without his leather jacket, bouncing around on his stocking feet—his big toe sticking out of a hole in the one sock.

"I won't forget you or what happened," the thug said. Brave words, but I noticed he kept his distance.

"I don't want you to forget," the bum said. "I want you to remember ... remember what happens if you pick on people." His voice was calm, quiet, but menacing. "Remember, if you come back here again, it won't just be your shoes and jacket that you lose." He held the rod up. "You have any idea what would have happened if I'd hit him in the head instead of the leg?"

Neither of them answered.

"You want to find out?" the man demanded as he stepped toward them, waving the rod in the air.

The two men hurried away.

"Come on back!" he yelled, but they kept moving, not looking back.

We stood there and watched as they limped off into the gathering darkness, the one with his arm around the other, helping him move. The sun was almost completely down and it was becoming darker by the second.

"Are you all right?" the bum asked.

"I'm okay … a little shaky … but okay … thanks." In truth I felt scared and confused and upset.

"Put on your shoes."

I bent down and slipped on the first shoe, untied the second, and put it on. My feet were cold and my socks wet. I quickly tied my laces up.

"What are you going to do with those?" I asked, pointing to the leather jacket and pair of boots lying on the ground beside me.

"I almost forgot." He picked up the jacket and tossed it into a garbage can. Next he grabbed one of the boots. "These are the sort of boots a soldier wears." He shook his head in disgust. "What an insult to soldiers … men prepared to sacrifice their lives to protect our country and save others' lives … even the lives of scum like those three. Come, I'll walk you out of the park."

I was going to say that wasn't necessary, but it was—I didn't want to walk alone, not now, after all that had happened, and certainly not in the dark. We walked along in silence. I wanted to say something to him. I didn't know exactly how to say it, but I had to try.

"It was lucky for me that you came along when you did," I said.

"Luck had nothing to do with it. This is not the best place to be, so I figured maybe it would be good for me to stay close, until you got out of the park."

"I didn't see you following me."

He laughed. "You weren't *supposed* to see me. I was off to the side, staying among the trees and bushes and shadows. If nothing happened you wouldn't have known I was ever there."

"But you thought something would happen."

"I thought something *could* happen," he answered. "I told you this place isn't safe ... especially not at night. It's good to have at least one friend with you—that's why I always carry this," he said, holding up the metal rod.

"I'm pretty happy you had that with you."

He shrugged. "Most people who live out here have something to protect themselves."

"People carry around pieces of metal?"

"Pieces of metal, pipes, box cutters, knives, machetes."

"People have machetes?" I questioned. I found that hard to believe.

He nodded. "They can be pretty deadly."

"I can't even imagine what it would do to somebody if you hit them with a machete."

"I don't have to imagine," he said, his words so quiet that I almost didn't hear him.

His answer startled me. Did that mean he didn't have to imagine because he'd seen it happen or because he'd done it himself? I edged slightly away from him. He'd saved me, but I didn't know anything about him other than he was some bum, a bum who carried a metal rod up his sleeve, a metal rod that he'd just used to smash some guy in the leg, maybe breaking it for all I knew. And worse still, he'd basically threatened to kill them if they came back ... *kill* them. What was to stop him from hitting *me* in the side of the head with it if I said something he didn't like, or if some crazy voice in his head told him to?

Up ahead I could see the street lights, and then flashes of cars passing by, and then finally the street itself. I felt a huge sense of relief. I'd be awfully happy to get out of that park and back onto the sidewalk. We stopped when we came to the street.

"You okay from here?" he asked.

"Sure, no problem. I really appreciate what you did. I don't know what would have happened if you hadn't come along."

"I have a pretty good idea," he said.

That sent a shudder up my spine. I had a pretty good idea too. "Thanks again for what you did."

"You want to really thank me?" he asked.

"Sure." I started to reach for my wallet.

"Don't pull that out," he snapped. "I don't want any more of your money. You already gave me some change."

"But I have more I could give to let you know how much I appreciate what—"

"The best thing you could give me—the way to thank me—is to *never* come to this park at night again. Okay?"

"You don't have to worry about that."

"Good. You'll be fine. Stay on the street. Do you have car to go now?"

"It's just up ahead."

"You better get going. The street is safer than the park, but that doesn't make it safe. Keep your eyes open and your head up, understand?"

I nodded. I wasn't going to let anybody sneak up on me again. I started off. I got partway down the block and then stopped and turned around. He was still standing there, watching—watching over me. I waved and he waved back. He turned and headed into the park. He quickly vanished into the darkness. Maybe he was just a bum. Maybe he was even crazy. But he'd been my guardian angel and he was gone. I suddenly felt open and exposed. I looked all around. I wondered if I was being watched. I hurried up the street.

Two

THERE WERE VERY FEW PEOPLE on the street, so I was surprised when I saw a line of people pressed against a building up ahead. I was just about to reach into my pocket and pull out the slip of paper that had the address written on it when it suddenly connected in my head—this was probably the place. As I got closer I saw a sign on the building—THE CLUB. The lettering was in bright orange paint, crudely done and peeling away.

The men in line, and I noticed that it *was* all men, were huddled together, like they were shielding each other from the wind and the cold. They stood unmoving, as still and silent as statues. As I walked by I became aware that not a single person reacted to my passing. Nobody said anything or even looked over. Their eyes were locked on the ground, staring at their feet. Nobody was making any eye contact with anybody else.

With them not looking at me I felt free to look at them. They were dressed in a shoddy assortment of coats and hats and scarves and boots and shoes. Nothing seemed to match anything else. It was obvious that some men had on layers and layers of clothing—they looked puffy. A couple weren't really even that badly dressed while some others looked as if they were clothed completely in rags, held together in defiance of gravity and sanity.

I stopped in front of a door that marked the start of the line. Should I wait or just go inside? I thought about it for a second. There was no way I was waiting out here with these people. Slowly, hesitantly, I walked to the door and gave it a little push. It opened and I peeked inside. The room was dominated by eight or ten long, long wooden tables, each flanked by benches. There wasn't a soul in sight. I edged in through the door. It was warm and there was the distinct smell of cooking. I wasn't sure what it was, but it didn't smell half bad.

A man wearing an apron and carrying a big pot came into the room through a swinging door down at the far end of the hall.

"Excuse me," I called out.

"It's almost ready, just wait outside and—" He looked up and saw me.

"I'm not here to eat," I explained. "I'm here to see Mr MacDonald."

"I'm MacDonald."

I walked over toward him. "I'm Ian Blackburn." I held out my hand to shake. He just stared at me, looking me up and down. I suddenly felt even more nervous and unsure of myself.

He turned away and put the pot down on a counter alongside another big pot. Both were steaming hot—that's where the smell was coming from.

"So why are you here?" he asked, sounding suspicious.

I lowered my hand. "I'm here to apply for a position."

He laughed. It was a thick, heavy, throaty laugh that forced its way out. "The only position we have is upright. Standing right here behind the counter shovelling out food."

"That's what I'm here for, to be interviewed to do that … as a volunteer."

"Volunteers we have, interviews we don't. You showed up so you get to work."

I felt relieved. Being late hadn't cost me the job. He reached down and grabbed something off the counter and tossed it to me. I unravelled it to reveal a balled-up apron. It was greyish and stained.

"Put it on and then slip on some gloves."

I started to take my coat off.

"Better leave that on. I ain't got time to lock it up in back and if you lay it down somebody might steal it … best not to lay anything down around here you don't want to walk. Some people might try to rip you off for a nice coat like that."

It wasn't much of a stretch for me to believe him. For a split second I thought of telling him what had happened and then stopped myself. I just felt embarrassed and stupid about the whole thing. I should have seen it coming.

I took a better look at him. He was a strange-looking old bird. He was shorter than me, but stocky, and looked like he could take care of himself. Actually, judging from the way his nose was all bent out of shape I was certain he'd been in more than a few fights in his time. I tried to figure out his age. His hair was grey and thin and his face was lined and weather-beaten. He had to be in his sixties, if not older.

I slipped the apron on over my head, looped the strings around my waist and tied them up.

"What did you say your name was again?" he asked.

"Ian."

"Well, Ian, I'll explain what you have to do. It isn't particularly complicated. Each man grabs one of those," he said, pointing to a pile of brown trays. "He puts a bowl and a plate and a plastic cup on it and then moves over here where you give him two scoops of food in the bowl, one slice of bread, and then I pour 'em a drink. Think you can handle that?"

"I think so."

"Some of the guys might ask you to give 'em more. Just tell 'em that they only get one serving. After everybody has eaten, if there's any left, then they can come back for seconds. Most of the fellas are regulars and know the rules, but some of 'em like to test anybody new."

"Okay, no problem, Mr. MacDonald."

"Call me Mac."

"Sure … Mac."

"So is this just a one-night thing or are you supposed to be here for a while?" he asked.

"Forty hours."

"Is this like a court-ordered thing?" Mac asked.

"Court-ordered … what do you mean?"

"You got convicted of something and were sentenced to do this instead of going to jail or paying a fine."

"No!" I exclaimed. "It's for school!" Did he think I looked like some sort of criminal?

"What sort of school?"

As he was talking he was wiping the counter and stirring the pot.

"My civics class. We have to do volunteer work to pass," I explained.

"So you *have* to be here."

"If I want to pass civics."

"This really isn't something you *want* to do," he said.

"Um … I guess not," I answered reluctantly, thinking that maybe I shouldn't have admitted that.

"You're not hoping to grow up to be a social worker or something like that, are you?" he asked. He sounded suspicious.

I laughed. "That's just about the *last* thing in the world I'd want to become." The truth was, there actually had been a time I'd toyed with that idea. Then my father told me how difficult the job was and how badly it paid.

"Even better! Some of these do-gooders who come around here to do volunteer work think they're here to save souls or do therapy instead of serving food." He paused and stared at me. "You're not here to judge 'em or save 'em, just serve 'em food."

"I'm not trying to save anybody except myself … from a failing mark," I said. "I'm just trying to do my hours so I can pass."

"Good. This ain't no social project. Understand?" He wiped his hands on a discoloured dishtowel tucked into his belt.

"You don't have to worry about me. I'm going to keep my mouth shut, serve food, do my hours, and leave."

He laughed again. "Sounds like you have a lot in common with the people here."

"What do you mean?" I asked.

"None of them want to be here either. And you're smart to keep your mouth closed. Worst thing you could do is ask a lot of questions. That sometimes leads to people getting upset."

"I'm not here to ask anybody anything," I said. "I won't even talk to anybody if you don't want me to."

"Talking is fine. Just don't be giving anybody any crap."

"I don't give crap." Unless somebody tries to give it to me first, I thought but didn't say.

"Just be polite and respectful. Don't go asking a whole lot of questions. Something you think might be innocent, just sort of making conversation—like where do you live—might set somebody off ... especially somebody who's paranoid. And almost everybody who walks through those doors is at least a little paranoid."

"Everybody?" I asked.

"You have to be at least a little paranoid if you want to survive living on the streets. There really are people out there who want to rip you off or hurt you. That's the way of the streets. Just remember, just 'cause somebody's paranoid doesn't mean they're not out to get him." He chuckled to himself. "I think it's time to let them in."

I watched as he walked over to the door and opened it up.

"Come on in, boys, supper's waiting!" he called out.

The first two men shuffled in and the line snaked in behind them. Mac stood by the door, welcoming people, shaking hands, patting people on the back. He gave one old man—all bent over and dressed in absolutely filthy clothes—a hug. I shuddered, wondering what sort of diseases and bugs the old man was carrying. My scalp got all itchy just thinking about it. As soon as I got home I was going to take one very long, very hot shower.

The first man stood in front of me, tray in hand. He was wearing a big bulky parka, a thick sweater, and a scarf wrapped around his neck, the standard toque on his head. He didn't look very old, maybe in his late twenties. Across the counter and through the steam and food smell rising from the pots I could still make out the distinct odour of alcohol coming off him.

"What are you serving?" he asked.

"Um ..." I didn't know. I lifted up the lid and peered in through the rising steam. "It looks like some sort of stew." I stirred it around with the big ladle and lifted a scoop. "Beef stew."

"Mac makes great stew. Ever try it?"

"No!" I exclaimed. Did he really think that I was going to eat food from a soup kitchen? "It's my first time here," I said, trying to cover up my feelings of disgust.

"If there's any left at the end, you should try it," he said.

"If there's any left, I will," I said, although I was just saying that to humour him.

I picked up the big ladle and dipped it in again. I carefully put some of the stew into the bowl on his tray. It actually did smell good. I repeated the process and the second scoop filled the bowl to the brim. The man reached out and grabbed a bun.

"Thanks," he said.

"You're welcome. I hope it's good."

"Guaranteed to be the *best* thing I eat today," he said and then chuckled. "Guaranteed to be the *only* thing I eat today."

"I'm … I'm … sorry," I stammered.

"Not your fault," he said and shrugged.

"Maybe you could take another bun or—"

He shook his head. "Can't do that. Might be taking the last bun away from somebody who gets nothing. Maybe at the end when you get some stew I'll get an extra bun."

"Sure … okay."

This really hadn't been what I'd expected. This guy hadn't even eaten today, and he was worried about somebody at the back of the line he probably didn't even know. That wasn't how I was expecting a street person to be.

"You two through gabbing?" barked the man behind him. "There are people here who need some grub, you know."

I startled and then quickly dipped the ladle into the pot. I fished out a heaping helping and as I dropped it into the bowl it slopped onto the tray.

"Be careful!" he barked. "Don't go wasting my food!"

"Sorry, it was an accident."

He was older and grizzled and there was more than just a *slight* odour of alcohol coming off him. He seemed to be swaying back and forth ever so gently, and as I carefully put a second scoop into his bowl I saw that the tray was shaking.

"You can take a bun," I said.

"You think I don't know the routine!" he snapped. "I've been coming here longer than you've been alive, you little—"

"Leave him alone, you old buzzard!" snapped the first man I'd served.

"You want a piece of me?" challenged the old man. "You hassle me and I'll cut ya!"

"Take your food, shut up, and sit down!" It was Mac. "You say another word and you'll be banned for two weeks!"

The old man opened his mouth to answer, revealing a mess of yellowed and missing teeth. He mumbled something under his breath, but turned and walked away, sitting down at the table with his back to us.

"Don't worry about it," Mac said to me. "You didn't do nothing wrong. Just keep serving."

I dipped the ladle back into the pot and served out food to the next man in line and then the next and the next. It was funny, every one of them was the same but different. Some were polite, others rude, some were like zombies, hardly noticing that I'd given them food until they were prodded by the person behind them to keep moving. There were those who were cursing under their breath or muttering away, talking to people I couldn't see or hear answer back. Some were angry. Others seemed cheerful, even happy. Maybe they were the craziest of the bunch. Wouldn't you have to be crazy to be happy eating at a soup kitchen and living on the street? There were some who didn't seem that much older than me, others who must have been in their seventies, and a whole bunch whose ages I couldn't discern behind the layers of grime, beard, and clothing. They could have been twenty-seven or seventy-two. Interestingly, there wasn't a woman in the group. Where did the shopping cart lady go to eat? Was there another soup kitchen for women?

I got to the bottom of the first pot. I was just going to put it aside when I looked back at the line. It was at least as long as when I'd started serving. What would happen if there wasn't enough food for the last few in line? I wasn't so worried about them going hungry as how they might react—how they might react to *me*—if they didn't get fed. What was that saying I'd heard about delivering bad news? *Kill the messenger* ... that was it. I'd be the guy to tell them there was no more food. That old man had mentioned cutting somebody and if the man in the park was to be believed everybody in here had some sort of weapon. That is, everybody in here but *me*.

I tipped the pot and scraped the stew off the side, accumulating it until there was a full ladle to dish out.

"That's the way you do it," Mac said. He had returned from the kitchen carrying more buns.

I put the now completely empty pot off to the side and dragged forward the second pot. I took off the lid. The stew was still steamy hot. Maybe I was hungrier than I thought because it did still smell good to me. I dipped in the ladle and added a second scoop to the bowl of the man patiently waiting. He smiled and nodded his head in thanks.

I caught a quick glimpse of my watch. I'd been here less than forty minutes. It seemed like hours already.

"Do we have enough?" I asked Mac, motioning toward the back of the line.

"I think we'll be okay. Hopefully enough that we get a bowl too. You already eaten?" Mac asked.

"I grabbed something before I left home," I answered. That something was a granola bar and a couple of cookies. I didn't care how good the stew smelled, or how hungry I was, there was no way I was going to eat here.

"You lyin' to me?" Mac asked.

"What?"

"You lyin' about eating?"

"No, of course not," I lied.

"Just wanted to make sure. Didn't want you to lie so you wouldn't be taking food away from some of our clients. We won't be taking food from somebody. We'll only eat once everybody has had their fill."

"It's just that I'm not hungry … honestly."

"How can you not be hungry for a bowl of this?" Mac asked in all seriousness. "It's my own recipe, made from only the finest ingredients."

"Where do you get all this food from?" I asked, trying to change the subject.

"Some I have to buy, but a whole lot of it comes from Second Harvest."

"What's that?" I asked as I continued to serve the people in line.

"It's an organization that picks up food from stores and restaurants that have extra. It's all perfectly good food that would go to waste if it wasn't collected and put to good use. The meat for our stew today is cut-up steak from Centros."

"Centros!"

"You know it?" he asked.

"Who doesn't? Centros is one of the classiest, most expensive restaurants in town."

"Never been there myself, but that's what I hear."

I'd been there half a dozen times with my parents. I thought it was best not to mention that.

"But why would they give away food?"

"Sometimes they order too much, or there's problems with the freezer, or the chef just doesn't think it's tender enough. Maybe they just want to do something good. Anyway you cut it, they get a charitable donation receipt and we get to feed some people who really need to be fed."

Just then there was a commotion over in the corner. Two men, sitting across from each other at a table, had jumped to their feet and were yelling and swearing at each other. It looked like it was going to evolve into a full-fledged fist fight.

"Excuse me," Mac said. He reached by me under the counter and pulled out a big black baseball bat! I backed away.

Mac moved around the counter and quickly got close to where the two men were screaming at each other. What was he going to do with that bat? Without warning he smashed the bat down on the table between the two men, causing cups to overturn and bowls and cutlery to jump along the whole length of the table!

"Both of you, sit down or get out!" he yelled at the top of his lungs.

The whole room had gone completely silent. Everybody had stopped eating or talking; they all stared at Mac holding the bat. Both men dropped back down to their seats without saying another word.

"How you act on the streets is your business!" Mac said sternly. "How you act in here is mine! I don't know what you were fighting about, but I want you both to forget it. Shake hands and be friends."

I expected them to argue or get up and leave. Instead they held out their hands and shook.

"That's better," Mac said. "We'll have no more of this ... from anybody." He looked around the room, holding the bat up. "Isn't life tough enough for us already? Aren't there enough people out there trying to harm and abuse you without doing it to each other?"

A couple of men called out in agreement and others nodded their heads. Mac walked back over, circled the counter, and put the bat away underneath it. The regular sounds of the room—talking, laughing, clinking of cutlery and bowls and glasses all started up again. It was like the whole thing had never taken place.

"Does that happen very often?" I asked.

"Too often for my liking, but not as much as in the past. I'm known to run a pretty strict place here. Those who aren't gonna follow the rules know better than to come here."

"If they don't come here where do they go instead?" I asked, hoping to avoid that place completely.

"This isn't the only location in town offering a meal. Of course, some people have been banned from some places and others don't ever come to soup kitchens to begin with."

"What do they do instead?" I asked.

"Eat out of dumpsters, hang around the streets or the park just over from here begging for change." He paused. "That park is one bad place."

Again I was tempted to say something but I held my tongue. I didn't know why I cared what he thought but I did. Maybe it was nothing more than me not wanting him to think I was an idiot or a wimp. I just kept on ladling out stew. If we did run out of food, at least I knew where the baseball bat was now.

Three

MAC GENTLY SHEPHERDED OUT the last of the men. As they'd eaten, people had become more animated and talkative and some had wanted to stay and talk to Mac. The very last few stragglers had been the most reluctant to leave. I guess I couldn't blame them. This wasn't the fanciest place in the world but at least it was warm and dry and inside. Mac said goodbye to the last man, closed the door and bolted it shut.

I continued to gather up bowls and cups, piling them up on a tray. I put two more bowls on the tray. It was now as full as I dared to carry. I hefted it up and carted it away, pushing through the swinging door and into the kitchen. It smelled better back here—smells of hot water and cooking odours. Out in the dining room the men were gone but their smell lingered on. Through the course of the evening, the smell of the food had been replaced by a foul combination of dirt and sweat and urine that stung my nostrils. It was so strong that it was more a taste than a smell.

On my first trip into the kitchen I'd been shocked to find out that nobody else was in the back helping. I'd figured that there had to be at least a couple of other people. There was nobody else. It had all been Mac and me—really Mac. If I hadn't showed up he would have done the whole thing by himself.

The counter was already overflowing with dirty dishes and I put down the tray carefully so as not to disturb the rest of the mess. The sink, filled with soapy suds, was already filled to capacity. Was I supposed to help wash the dishes as well? I hated washing dishes—not that I did it very often. Berta, our housekeeper, took care of all those things. If I was supposed to do the dishes here that could take forever. Then again, what did I care? The longer I was here the more quickly I'd be through having to come back. It was seven forty-five. If I worked another fifteen minutes that would be two hours. That meant I had to come here *twenty* times to complete my placement. If I came here three times a week that would take almost seven weeks. If I hadn't been so stupid I would have started doing my hours when everybody else did. It would probably be better if I did stay and work on the dishes. If I stayed until nine that would be three hours, and I'd only have to come here thirteen times—only thirteen times. I shook my head.

I dipped my hands into the hot water and fished around for the dishcloth. I swirled it around the first bowl—the first of how many bowls? I didn't even want to count them. Satisfied that the first bowl was clean, I dipped it into the second sink, which was filled with clear water, and rinsed off the remaining suds.

"You don't have to do that," Mac said as he entered the kitchen carrying more dishes.

"Somebody's got to do it," I said and shrugged.

"That somebody's usually me."

"Do you do everything around here?" I asked as I pulled out another bowl.

"I'm the executive director, the chief cook, the bouncer and bottle washer." He set the tray down. "Although sometimes I have more help than I want."

"What do you mean?"

"Sometimes there's a tidal wave of do-gooders who show up. They can cause more damage than they do good. You didn't do half bad tonight," he said as he continued to stack bowls.

"So does that mean I did half good?"

"Don't push it. What that means is you didn't screw up and that means you can come back again."

"Gee, thanks, what an honour."

"Maybe you *should* consider it an honour. Lots of people I don't ask to come back. You done okay. You served the food, you didn't ask too many questions, you were polite, and like I said, you were here for the same reason as everybody else—you had no choice … same as everybody we fed tonight. I never met anybody who said his dream was to live on the streets, beg for change, wonder where his next meal was gonna come from, or where he was going to sleep." He dropped more bowls in the sink. "If you didn't have to do this for school, is there any way in the world you'd be here tonight?"

I laughed. "Yeah, right, like washing dishes is my dream job."

"That's another thing I like about you," he said. "You're honest."

I didn't know what to say to that. I didn't know if my parents or most of my teachers would have thought that about me.

"What about you?" I asked. "Do *you* want to be here?"

"This is the place I'm *supposed* to be."

I guess I looked confused, because that was how I felt.

"This is my calling."

"You sound like a priest or minister or something," I said. I focused on the dishes in the sink, not wanting to look at him as the conversation got more serious.

"Maybe I am."

"You are?"

"Don't sound so surprised. Don't I seem like a minister?" he asked, a serious look on his face.

I thought about the minister at our church—the church we went to at Christmas and Easter and maybe two other times a year. He was always dressed immaculately, with a sharp crease in his pants, drove a fancy car, and lived in the big beautiful house beside the church. Sometimes my father would go golfing with him at the country club. I could picture our minister on the golf course, and I could clearly see him standing up at the altar boring me with another sermon. What I couldn't do was imagine him making stew or cleaning tables. I certainly couldn't, in my *wildest* dreams, picture him pulling out a baseball bat to stop a fight between two of the parishioners.

"Well?" Mac asked.

"Not really," I admitted, hoping I wasn't insulting him.

"I'll take that as a compliment," he said as his serious expression dissolved into a crooked smile. "I'm not part of any church or anything like that, but this is my mission.

God is everywhere. Here," he said, motioning with his hands. "And out there on the streets."

I don't know which streets he'd been on but the ones I'd walked down today looked like God had forgotten them and the people who lived on them.

"How long have you been doing this?" I asked, turning away from the soapy sink.

"It's coming up to ten years I've been running the place. Seven days a week."

"Seven days a week?" I asked in amazement. "Don't you get any time off?"

"People need to eat seven days a week. I'll take a day off when hunger does. This is my place … literally." He pointed to a bed in the corner.

"You mean you live here?" I asked incredulously.

"Saves on the commute and the rent is perfect. I've slept in a lot worse places."

I wanted to ask him what could possibly be worse than this, but I didn't want to offend him. I kept washing dishes, rinsing them off, and piling them on the counter. Mac took each one, dried it off, and put it in the cupboard. There didn't seem to be an end to the bowls.

"How many people you figure were here tonight?" I asked. "It must have been close to a hundred."

"One hundred and seven," he said. "I have to do a head count. Our funding is based on the number of people that get fed."

"I thought the food came from fancy restaurants."

"That and food donations from all over, but they don't pay the rent, or my salary, or guarantee there's food on the table every night. We get some funds from the government and some from the United Way. These people need food every night."

"I had no idea there were that many homeless in the city. One hundred and seven seems like a lot," I said.

"That's just a little drop in the bucket. Those are the people who showed up here tonight. It doesn't include them who skipped a meal, or went to another soup kitchen, or got their meal from a dumpster behind McDonald's, or were too drunk to show up, or who were spending the night in jail or in an emergency department of a hospital, or who were off their medication and couldn't stand to be around other people," he said, counting the reasons off on his fingers.

"Then how many people—homeless people—do you think there are in the city?"

"It varies from month to month, mostly depending on the season, and whether you count kids who run away for a day or two," he explained.

"Right now, *tonight,* how many people do you think are out there on the streets looking for a place to sleep?" I didn't know why but it seemed important to me.

He didn't answer right away. I could tell he was thinking. "My guess is well over a thousand ... maybe two thousand."

"That can't be right," I argued. "Sure, I see some street people around but there can't be two thousand."

"You don't live around here, do you?"

I shook my head. "About a thirty-minute drive away in the suburbs." I wanted to say in another universe but I didn't.

"Not many street people where you live, I bet. Lots here if you know where to look. You'd see 'em too, if you went out with me on my rounds."

"Your rounds?"

"I walk through the streets and alleys and parks, talking to people, letting them know about the kitchen here, and suggest places where they might want to sleep."

"Is that a safe thing to do?" My experience in the park came flooding back.

"It's safe … for me. I know pretty well everybody. It's not like I'm a stranger."

"I guess you really do get to know a lot of them," I said, remembering how he greeted people at the door this evening as they came in.

"I know a lot of them," he repeated in agreement. "I even understand them … well, at least some of them. You know, we're all the same in so many ways, but I don't pretend to know the demons that some people live with. You can walk a mile in somebody's shoes but those shoes still belong to them." He paused. "It's getting late. How are you getting home?"

I hadn't really thought about it. "I guess I should call and ask my mother to pick me up."

"Then why don't you call now. By the time we get finished she should be here. The phone is right over there."

I dried my hands on the apron and walked over to the phone.

"And tell her to make sure she keeps all the car doors locked," Mac said.

That sounded like good advice.

Four

THE SOUND OF THE CHALK squeaking against the board brought me out of my thoughts and back into the classroom. Mrs. Watkins was writing something. I'd been trying my best to block her out all class but she had the same grating effect as the chalk. She seemed to know just what to say or how to say it to stop me from drifting off too often. Maybe that was a good quality for a teacher to have but it certainly cut down on my ability to catch up on my sleep.

It had been late when I got to bed and even later when I finally drifted off. My mind was filled with all the images I'd seen the night before. My mother would have called it processing. Leave it to her to put everything in computer terms instead of human terms—computers she knew about. I lay in bed thinking about the lady with the shopping cart, the men shuffling in for their meal, the conversations—angry, crazy, polite—and the smells of the food and the alcohol and the body odours. And I realized how close I came to not only losing my shoes, but maybe having the crap beaten out of me, and wondering what could have happened if that man hadn't stopped them.

Mrs. Watkins moved aside to reveal the words she had written on the board. In big letters they read

Peacekeepers, not War Makers.

"Does anybody know what that means?" she asked.

"It probably means more work for us," a voice shot out from the back of the room and a number of people laughed in response.

"Anybody else care to add something ... something of value?" she asked.

Nobody raised a hand or a voice.

"Does the name Lester B. Pearson mean anything?" Mrs. Watkins asked.

"Didn't he used to play for the Leafs?" the same guy—Jeremy—asked and there was more laughter.

"Somebody better come up with an answer or everybody is going to be given an additional assignment on Canadian prime ministers," she threatened.

"Okay, he was a Canadian prime minister," somebody answered.

"And he is best known for?" Mrs. Watkins questioned.

Obviously he wasn't best known for much of anything because nobody even knew who he was.

Mrs. Watkins let out a big, deep sigh. "Let's try this from another angle. In the rest of the world what is *Canada* known for? What are the symbols or institutions or objects that the world thinks of when it thinks of Canada and Canadians?"

"Hockey," several people called out.

"We're the best in the world on the ice. Everybody knows that," Jeremy said.

"What else?" Mrs. Watkins asked.

"Maple syrup and the Mounties," somebody else volunteered.

"Universal health care," Kelsey added.

"All sorts of programs including medicine, pensions, and education," Mrs. Watkins said, nodding. "What else?"

"The paint roller," a boy—Justin—offered.

"Paint roller?" the kid behind me repeated, sounding amused.

"A Canadian invented it," the first boy explained and shrugged.

"All valid. Now, what else?" Mrs. Watkins asked.

"Snow and cold and igloos and Eskimos," another girl added.

"Niagara Falls and the mountains," another voice added.

"All good. And are we seen as a country that believes in war?"

"I hope not," somebody said, "because I don't think we even have an army."

"We have armed forces. Not large but very professional and well respected," Mrs. Watkins said. "The question was, do we believe in war?"

"We were in both world wars," Kelsey said hesitantly.

"We were a major player," Mrs. Watkins confirmed. "And there was the Korean War and the Gulf War, but the question isn't have we *been* in wars but do we *believe* in war?" Mrs. Watkins said. "What do you think, Ian?"

I jumped at the mention of my name. That was one of her annoying, chalk-like qualities, calling out your name when you thought you were being left alone.

"Well?" she asked, looking directly at me.

"I'm not really sure … but I guess not really. We're peaceful," I said. I looked at the words looking back at me on the board. "We're peacekeepers not war makers."

"Exactly!" she exclaimed. "Now who was Lester B. Pearson?"

"I thought we'd answered that one already," Justin said. "He was a prime minister."

"But what else?" she demanded.

"Maybe he was the one who started us being peacekeepers," I offered.

"Right again!" Mrs. Watkins exclaimed. "He put forward a plan, when he was foreign minister, to send peacekeepers to the Middle East. These peacekeepers were almost all Canadians and they separated the two warring sides, averting a war in the Suez. And after the success of this first mission he created the legacy of peacekeeping that has marked Canada's role on the international scene and saved literally hundreds of thousands of lives around the world."

That did sound impressive … well, not to me, but I'm sure to some people.

"For his efforts he was awarded the Nobel Prize for Peace in 1957," she continued. "He was subsequently elected by the United Nations as—" Her words were cut off by the loud ringing of the bell marking the end of class. Everybody, en masse, grabbed their books and bags and rose to their feet.

"I want everybody to read their textbooks, pages 145 to 155 tonight!" Mrs. Watkins yelled out over the din. "There just might be a test tomorrow!"

I'd try and remember—maybe I should write it down. There was no point in doing these volunteer hours if I didn't at least pass the rest of the course. I pulled out my pen and started to write myself a reminder on my hand.

"You should try using paper," Mrs. Watkins suggested. "It's a wonderful new invention. I think it was the Chinese created it … about three thousand years ago."

"At least I'm writing it down," I replied.

"I guess you're right. So how did things go at your placement … you did go, didn't you?" she asked.

"I went and things went okay."

"Just okay?"

"The placement was fine. It was just that it was, I don't know, *different*."

"Different as in not what you are used to or not what you were expecting?"

"Both."

"I'm sure it was all pretty overwhelming."

I nodded. "It was. It all just kept going around and around in my head after I left. I even had trouble concentrating in class today."

"Well, at least you had a valid excuse for not concentrating today." She smiled. "Cheap shot. Seriously, it really is a different world out there, isn't it?"

"Not a different world. A different *universe*."

"That's what this course is designed to do, to open your mind up to other perspectives. So when do you go back?" she asked.

"Friday night. I'm going to help with set-up, then dinner, then help clean up."

"If you need to talk about things, feel free to give me a call," she said.

"A call … like on the phone?"

"That would be the right way. I'm in the book if you need to talk."

"You want me to call you at home?" This was all very strange. I didn't even think she liked me and now she was offering to let me call her at home. I got the feeling that a whole lot of teachers didn't even want to talk to me when I was in class.

"A big part of my course is asking you to move beyond the classroom. It would be very hypocritical of me to ask you to do that while I stayed safely within the confines of my class. If you need to call, then call."

"I'll be fine."

"I'm sure you'll handle it." She paused for a few seconds. "Just remember, a sign of strength is asking for help."

Strength or weakness, it didn't matter because I wasn't going to be calling her at home.

"I've got to tell you that I was most impressed, and somewhat surprised, with your decision to pursue that particular placement. Most kids went for the easy stuff—reading to kids in a local elementary school, or going to the humane society to walk dogs, or even visiting seniors at the local nursing home."

She'd described most of the placements my friends were doing.

"Not that there's anything wrong with those placements," she said. "They all make a contribution. What you're doing, though, is different. Almost noble. Now you better get going or you're going to be late for your next class."

Five

"ARE YOU SURE you have to do this?" my mother asked as we drove along.

"Are you sure you want me to pass civics?"

"There have to be more pleasant places in a better part of town where you could have done your hours."

I had to agree that *pleasant* and *better* certainly weren't words that I'd use to describe either the soup kitchen or the streets that surrounded it.

"I started it so I'm going to finish it."

"I just wish you hadn't started it working at a place like that."

That would have been my wish as well—unfortunately most of what I wished for didn't come true. At least one of the few benefits this placement had was that it offended my mother. She always liked things to be so proper. So precise, so tidy and organized. This was none of those things. That it bothered my mother almost made up for me having to give up a Friday night—almost. I'd rather be out with my friends but I had to do the hours as soon as possible.

It was a shame I didn't get credit for the time I'd spent thinking about the soup kitchen or I'd have already been through with my community hours. I couldn't get it out of my mind. And the more I thought about it, the less real it all seemed. It was like I'd watched a movie about it instead of actually being there.

Tonight I was dressed better. By that, I mean I dressed *worse*—old coat, as close to beat up as I could find. It sort of belonged to my father. It was what he used to wear when he did yard work—at least when he used to do yard work. It had been years since he'd cut the grass or raked leaves or shovelled the snow. Now there was a landscape company that did all of that. And another company that took care of the pools, and another that washed the windows. He was far too busy—and too important—to do any of those jobs. Now if he could just find somebody to parent, he wouldn't have to show up at all.

I had also dug up an old pair of sneakers. They were scuffed up and worn out. I was sure nobody would want to steal them, and if they did I'd gladly give them up without a fight.

"I still don't know why you couldn't have dressed a bit better," my mother said, repeating the refrain I'd heard since she first saw my outfit.

"Like I said, it's better to dress down. If I look like I might have money, then somebody might want to try and get that money from me."

"Then by all means just give them a dollar or two so they'll leave you alone," she said. "Your father always gives those squeegee kids a dollar so they won't scratch up his car. It's not like we can't afford it."

"Can we afford for me to have my wallet ripped off, or my shoes or jacket stolen, or for me to be bashed over the head?"

"Please, Ian, don't be so dramatic."

"I'm *not* being … Fine … whatever."

I was tempted to tell her what had happened the other night in the park, but I stopped myself. I'd save that for later and spring it on her at just the right time.

"And it's such a long distance from home, such a long way to drive," she said.

"Sorry to inconvenience you," I said icily.

"It's not that."

"You don't even have to drive me. I can get there and back on my own. If it's such a big hassle, I can take the subway home tonight."

"Not from this part of the city and certainly not at night."

I was so happy she said that. I'd only been bluffing. A drive was a lot nicer, and safer. They'd just have to keep driving me places until I got my licence and my own car—that was the reason I was going in the first place. It was important not to lose sight of that.

"You can let me off anywhere along here," I suggested. We were within a block now.

"I'll drop you off right out front where I picked you up the other night. I'd rather not have you on these streets by yourself."

"I can take care of myself."

"You think you can take care of yourself, but you have no idea what goes on in this part of town."

"Sure, fine, whatever."

Actually I was a little embarrassed to be driven up to a soup kitchen in a Mercedes that probably cost more than all the meals that had been served there for the past year

I grabbed a toque off the seat and pulled it low over my ead. It was an old ratty one and it was a tight fit … lthough it certainly would help me fit in down here. Was some sort of rule that every street person had to wear a oque?

My mother pulled the car over to the curb directly in ont of the building. There was no lineup in front—I'd een hoping that was the case. It was still early—not even ve o'clock—and I was here to help with the set-up.

"You'd think they could do something about this ace," my mother said. "Fix it up a little or—"

"They spend their money on other things … like food r the street people."

"I just think a little bit of paint wouldn't cost much and would certainly improve the image."

"Appearances don't mean that much down here," I said.

"Judging from *your* appearance that's pretty obvious."

"I think they believe it isn't what you look like, but hat you do." I opened the car door and climbed out.

"Call when you know what time—"

I slammed the door shut, using the fine German engi-ering of the car to close *her* out. I turned and walked ay without looking back. I'd gone no more than a few ps when I heard the car pull away, leaving behind a all squeal of rubber on the pavement. She was obvi-sly mad. Good. It shouldn't just be me who was mad all time.

I grabbed the handle of the door to the Club and tried pull it open. It rattled but didn't open. I knocked. It hoed loudly. I waited, listening for an answer. There s none. I knocked again. This time louder and longer.

Still nothing. I'd be awfully ticked off if I'd come dow
here early—like we'd agreed—and Mac wasn't here
Either way, though, whether I was in there working or ou
here standing, I was still counting this as volunteer hours
I knocked again. No answer. Either Mac wasn't here or h
was just ignoring the noise. He probably got a lot o
people pounding on the door wanting to get inside to ea
It wasn't like most of the homeless people had watche
Maybe there was another way in.

I circled around to the alley at the side of the buildin
I'd gone no more than a few feet when I was stopped i
my tracks by the sight of two legs sticking out fro
beside a dumpster. Was somebody dead or … I gave m
head a shake. It was probably just somebody waiting f
supper. They would have figured this was a good place
get out of the wind. I walked forward, angling out ar
away from that side of the alley. I glanced over and the
stopped for a better look. It was an old man, sitting on th
ground, leaning against the wall, his eyes closed, a hal
empty bottle in his hand. As I stood there, he opened o
eye and looked at me. He mumbled something I couldn
hear and then his eye fell shut again. He certainly wasn
dead. Not unless you counted dead drunk.

As I got to the end of the alley I saw a large truc
backed in so it was tucked close to the open rear door
the building. At that instant Mac came out through t
door and grabbed a box from the back of the truck. H
looked up, saw me, and waved.

"Just in time!" he called out. "Grab a box!"

I rushed over. The truck was piled high with crates a
cardboard boxes and bins. I picked one up.

"What's in all of these?" I asked.

"This is a place where people come to get food … so …"

"This is all food?"

"Bingo!"

I trailed after Mac, and as we entered the building a nan came out.

"Extra hands is good," he said. He had on a shirt mblazoned with Second Harvest Trucking on the front so assumed he was the driver.

Mac set his box down on the table that was already iled high with other boxes. I went to put mine down vhen he stopped me.

"That one goes in the freezer. Follow me, I'll show ou."

Mac led the way to a large metal door. He opened it up nd gestured for me to enter. I was immediately hit with a vave of cold. It was a gigantic walk-in freezer. The walls vere lined with shelves and the shelves were filled with oxes and cartons and containers.

"Put it right here," Mac said.

"There's a whole lot of food in here."

"Enough for eight or nine days."

"There's got to be more than that."

"Second time here and the kid thinks he's an expert," ac said.

"No, it's just that—"

Mac started laughing, his breath coming out in little hite puffs in the cold. "You gotta lighten up, kid. I was st pulling your leg."

We walked out of the freezer and he closed the door hind us with a loud metallic click.

"It takes a lot of food to feed more than a hundred men a day," Mac said. "A lot of food and a whole lot of work. Glad to see you here to help. Although I'm a little surprised."

"Why are you surprised? This is when I'm supposed to be here, right?"

"That's the time we agreed to, but lots of people who show up once don't show up again. Especially people who aren't used to this sort of thing ... people who come from privilege."

"What makes you think that's me?" I asked.

"Well, for starters, the way you were dressed last time in that expensive coat and shoes. You made a better choic this time," he said.

"I thought I could fit in better this way," I admitted feeling a bit embarrassed. "But lots of people own a coa like the one I was wearing. That doesn't mean my famil is rich."

"Maybe not the coat, but certainly the Mercedes tha picked you up. That one probably cost more than hundred grand, right?"

I nodded my head. It was one of the top-of-the-lir cars. But how did he know what sort of car picked me up Had he been spying on me?

"I was watching when you left, peeking out th window, to make sure you got picked up safe," Mac sai answering my unspoken thoughts.

"Doesn't matter what car picked me up or dropped m off," I said, feeling a bit defensive. "All that matters is th I have to put in my hours, so I'm here."

Mac laughed. "Like I said before, that's one of th things I like about you, kid. You aren't going to give m ome crap about helping the poor. You're here to do a job. Ionest. I like that. But you know, there are other places vhere you could have done your hours. You could have veaseled out of being here."

"That's what my mother wanted me to do."

"But you didn't do what she wanted. How come?"

I considered giving him a completely honest answer; hardly ever did what my mother or father wanted nless I had no choice. "I told you I'd be here so I'm ere," I said. That wasn't a complete lie.

"Good. How about if you continue unloading the truck hile I finish up making supper. Unless you want to do e cooking and I'll do the unloading?"

"I think I'll do the unloading. Lifting I know how to). Cooking for a hundred people I don't."

"Same as cooking for two people. Just multiply all the gredients by fifty."

I went out to continue unloading. Each time I came in ith a box I caught a glimpse of Mac working at the ove. It wasn't just that I didn't know how to cook for one ndred people. I didn't know how to cook for two. Or en one. I'd never needed to. Berta did all of that.

Berta was my nanny when I was a baby, and then hen I didn't need a nanny any more she became our usekeeper and organizer. She had an apartment in our sement and she was always there. My mother said rta was sort of like the family's *wife* who took care of the day-to-day business of running our household. I ln't think of her as anybody's wife, but she was family. e'd always been there. She was there when I came me from school. Because of her, the house was never

empty, and because my father and mother were always s
busy with business meetings and travel and of cours
social things, it *would* have been empty without her. Fille
with lots of expensive things—but empty. I couldn
even imagine what it would be like without Bert
around—thank goodness I'd never known and I'd neve
have to know.

I guess it also worked out for Berta. She was originall
from Guatemala and that's where all her family still live
so I guess in some ways we were like her family too.

I'd once started to figure out how often I ate with m
parents and how often it was just me and Berta for dinne
I looked back for two or three weeks and then stoppe
There was no point in quantifying what I already kne
Not that there was anything wrong with eating with Bert
I liked eating with her. I liked being with her.

She had a soft, gentle laugh, and she always seem
to know what questions to ask and, just as importa
what questions not to ask. Those were the times I to
her the rest of the story anyway. I knew I could trust h
She didn't judge me, although she did offer advice
softly spoken with her lilting accent. I loved her acce
My parents told me that when I was little I spo
English with a Spanish accent. That shouldn't ha
been a surprise since she'd spent more time with
than my mother did.

"Much more to go?" Mac asked.

"Almost done."

"Good. When you're finished, you can start bringi
out the plates and cups and utensils."

"Sure. By the way, what's for supper tonight?" I ask

"Spaghetti with meat sauce." Mac lifted the lid on the biggest pot I'd ever seen. He grabbed a wooden spoon—a spoon that was about the same size as a canoe paddle—and stirred the bright red sauce that was bubbling away. He needed to use both hands to move the contents.

"I make sure there's lots and lots of vegetables in the sauce," Mac said. "Best thing to protect 'em from getting scurvy."

"Scurvy? Isn't that what sailors got in the old days ... you know ... like Christopher Columbus?"

"Yep. Being at sea for a long time without fruits and vegetables does that."

"And street people get it?" I asked.

"They don't get what you'd call a balanced diet. Speaking of which, have you eaten?" Mac asked.

I hadn't and it was too early to claim I had. I shook my head.

"Finish up and I'll set out two bowls before we let the crowd in. Okay?"

"You sure there'll be enough for everybody?" I asked.

"There will be, but that's mighty nice of you to ask."

I WAS IN CHARGE of serving the spaghetti. I was using a big pair of serving tongs. Mac was putting on the sauce. His job was way easier. The noodles were hard to get out of the pot and onto the plate. It almost seemed like they were alive and struggling to stay in the pot so they wouldn't be eaten. And when I did convince the noodles to leave, it was hard to get just the right amount, the right serving size. If I put on too much, I couldn't very well reach out and take it back, and if I didn't put out enough,

I could get somebody mad. It was much simpler serving the stew the other night—two scoops, plop, plop.

An old grizzled man stood in front of me, tray in hand. I wondered how old he was. I was finding that everybody looked old and worn. He could have been fifty but he could have been one hundred and fifty.

"Is it any good?" he asked.

"It's really good," I answered. It was good enough for me to have eaten two full servings.

"It don't smell right."

I thought it smelled pretty good. "It's the garlic in the sauce you're smelling."

"They put somethin' in the sauce?" he asked.

"There's lots of things. Garlic, green peppers, onions and—"

"Says who?" the old man demanded.

"Well … me, I guess."

"And who are you and who do you work for?" the old man snapped.

I didn't know what to say. The old man started to snarl, his teeth—those that he had—yellowed and crooked and grubby, were locked together in a fierce-looking grimace, and he started to make a strange noise. Was he growling?

"What did you put in that sauce?" he yelled. He raised his fist and started shaking it toward me.

I backed a half step away. I felt a rush of adrenaline surge through my body. I realized that everybody had stopped talking or shuffling or eating and all eyes were on us.

"I didn't put anything in the—"

"It's okay," Mac said, stepping forward and cutting me off.

"How do I know it ain't poisoned?" the old man demanded. "How do I know this ain't another plot to get me and everybody else in here?" He gestured around the room.

"Come on, buddy, you've been coming here a long time. You know I wouldn't poison you or let anybody else poison you," Mac reasoned. "You *know* me."

The old man stopped growling and he lowered his fist. Those had to be good signs. He looked at Mac, long and hard, like he was trying to figure out if what he was saying was true. His grimace dissolved into a twisted, broken smile like he'd suddenly realized that it was Mac. I felt myself relax.

That had looked like it was going to end really bad, and Mac had managed to handle it so that—

"How do I know it's you?" the old man demanded. "How do I know they didn't kill the *real* Mac and replace him with you when they poisoned the food? How do I know you're not an alien!" he yelled. He raised his fist and started to growl again. If he wasn't so old and frail and if Mac wasn't here I would have been afraid. Actually, I was afraid. I'd never seen anybody this crazy this close up.

"Would I poison myself?" Mac said, his voice calm and quiet. He reached into the pot and grabbed a noodle, stuffing it in his mouth. Next he took a spoon, dipped it in the sauce, and took a sample.

"See?" Mac said.

Once again the man lowered his fist and the growling was replaced by a throaty, scratchy laugh.

"Mac … it's you … right?"

"Who else would be stupid enough to be here, you old buzzard?"

The old man held out his hand and they shook.

"Go ahead," Mac said, "serve him."

The old man held out his tray. Carefully, very carefully, I put on some spaghetti.

"Thank you so much, young man," he said sweetly.

Next Mac poured on sauce—giving him an extra big serving—and the man shuffled off to eat.

"Thanks," I said to Mac.

"No problem. That's why I'm here. Sometimes you just gotta enter their heads and figure out what they're thinking."

"I can't believe that. He actually thought you were an alien. An alien who was here to poison him."

"That's why I had to sample the sauce to prove him wrong," Mac explained.

"But what I don't understand is if he thought you were an alien, isn't it possible that what poisons humans isn't going to hurt an alien?" I asked.

"Ssshhhhhh!" Mac hissed. "Let's not give anybody else any ideas!"

"That's good advice," another voice said.

I looked up to the man standing in front of me holding out his tray. It was the man from the park!

"Good to see you!" Mac exclaimed and the two men shook hands over the counter. "Haven't seen you for a while. Good to have you back. How've you been?" Mac asked.

"I'm fine. More important, how is your food today?"

"Good as always," Mac said. "See for yourself. Ian, give the Sarge a big serving 'cause he's a big guy."

"The same as everybody else would be fine," he said softly.

I pulled out a blob of spaghetti. As it had been getting colder it had become increasingly more difficult to manage. Whether he wanted it or not, he was getting a bigger serving.

"Thank you. I see you have on a different jacket today. I trust that was a choice and not something forced on you."

"I thought it was smarter to wear this when I'm around the neighbourhood."

"Wise move."

"Do you two know each other?" Mac asked.

"We met briefly in the park," the man said. "He kindly offered me some spare change. He's a nice young man."

"Yeah, I think he's a keeper," Mac said.

"I'm sure he is. *Merci* to you both." He nodded his head and then walked off looking for a seat. I watched as he walked. There was no shuffle or stagger in his step. His back was as straight as a rod. He looked more like he was marching than walking.

"You called him Sarge," I said.

"That's what everybody calls him. It's not his name. That's just what we call him. He was in the army before is what I heard."

That would explain the way he walked, the way he held himself—the way he knocked that man down and wielded that iron bar.

"So he was a sergeant?"

"Might have been," Mac said with a shrug. "He gets called Sarge the way somebody who used to drive a taxi might be called Cabby. Everybody here has a nickname and a story," Mac said.

"And what's his story?" I asked.

"What I know I'll tell you sometime." Mac paused. "That is, if you tell me the rest of the story about you and him meeting. I get the feeling that there's more there."

I nodded my head. "It's a deal."

Six

I REMOVED THE STOPPER from the sink and the water started to swirl away. I pulled off the bright yellow gloves that Mac had made me wear. He'd said that if I was going to be here on a regular basis he didn't want me filing a workman's compensation complaint about having dishpan hands.

"You all finished in here?" Mac yelled out.

"Pretty well. You?" He'd been working out front sweeping and wiping the tables and getting things ready for tomorrow's meal.

"All done. So you got a ride home?" he asked.

"I'll call to arrange it." I paused. "You were going to tell me about that man … Sarge."

"Not tonight."

"Why not?" I asked.

"Not enough time."

"I could tell them to pick me up later."

"Not your time, mine. I've got to get going."

"You got a big date?" I asked.

"I should be so lucky. I'm heading out onto the streets to do my rounds."

"What exactly do you do out there?" I asked.

"Hard to explain, really." He hesitated. "But I could show

you some time … if you were interested in coming along."

"Sure, that would be good," I answered. I was interested, but also more than a little uneasy. Going out there would be a little like riding a roller coaster or watching a scary movie—neither of which I liked doing.

"You know, it would give you hours on your community service."

Mac knew which buttons to push.

"I could come tonight," I said. The words had jumped out before I'd thought them through.

"It'll be almost midnight before I'm through," he warned.

"It's a Friday night. I don't have to be in until later than that."

"What about your ride?" Mac asked.

"I'll tell them to come and get me later. I'd like to come … you know, it *would* be some more hours. Quicker I do them the sooner I'm done."

He didn't answer right away. I didn't know if I should be happy or disappointed no matter what answer he gave.

"You make the call, just to make sure, and you can come with me. You know where the phone is."

"Yeah." I wandered out of the main part of the kitchen and into the little alcove that Mac had made into his home. It held his bed and a small TV and a few personal items sitting on top of his dresser. Unbelievably, this was his house and it wasn't nearly as big as our pool cabana. What would my parents think if they saw this? There was no worry there. They'd never see it. They'd never know and wouldn't care to know.

I picked up the phone—old, black, with a dial—like an

antique. I dialed the number. It rang and rang and—

"Good evening, Blackburn residence."

"Hi, Berta, it's me."

"Hello, *Eon*."

That's how she always said my name—it wasn't *Ian,* it was *Eon*. I liked the way she said it.

"Can I speak to my mother or father?" I asked.

"They are both still out, Eon."

"Out? My mother knew I was going to be calling about now to get a ride home."

"She asked me to come and get you when you called. If you can give me directions I can—"

"I don't want a ride yet. It'll be a couple more hours, maybe three. I have more work to do."

"You can call when you're ready. I'm just here. I'll come for you."

"Thanks, Berta." I could always count on *her*.

"You be careful, *carino mio*."

"I will. Goodbye. I'll call later." I put the phone down.

Carino mio ... that was Spanish for "my dearest." That's what she called me all the time when I was little. Now she only said that to me when there was nobody around to hear. It still made me smile.

"It's all set," I said as I rejoined Mac.

He already had his jacket on and had a red backpack over his shoulder. I grabbed my coat off the peg behind the door.

"Let's get rolling," Mac said.

We left through the back door. It was chilly, especially after the misty, steamy warmth of the kitchen. The air smelled fresh—well, at least as fresh as air could be in the back alley in a big city. It was certainly better than the odours inside—that strange mixture of cooking and cleaning, sweat and grime, clothes that had been lived in, slept in and soiled.

Mac put a big padlock on the door and snapped it shut. He started walking but rather than heading up the alley toward the street, he followed the alley in the other direction … away from the street lights.

"Cold tonight," Mac said and he gave a little shiver.

It was chilly.

"It's supposed to go down almost to freezing tonight," Mac said. "I always need to know what the temperature is going to be. A few degrees can mean the difference between life and death."

"How?" I asked.

"People who fall asleep outside can freeze to death."

"Do people really freeze to death in this city?" I asked skeptically.

"Every year one or two people. This year six."

"Come on … really?"

"Really."

"It's just that I've never heard anything about it."

"Homeless people dying don't make the front page of the paper or the lead story on the evening news. It's always buried in the back … the way they lead their lives. You remember saying you didn't believe how many homeless there are in the city?"

"Yeah," I said, feeling defensive.

"You're not seeing 'em because you're not looking for 'em. You have to spend time in the places you're not supposed to go … places you'd be smart to stay away from … places like the one we're going to go tonight."

We walked along in silence for a while.

"So tell me," Mac said, "how do you know Sarge?"

"I met him last night when I came down to do my volunteer hours," I said. "Met him in one of those places I'm probably not supposed to go. I was cutting across Selby Park and—"

"Selby Park! That wasn't very bright. It's not safe for you to be in there!"

"I didn't know that then. I know it now."

"Did something happen?" Mac asked.

I was tempted to leave some parts out—the parts that made me look stupid or weak—but if I'd done that there wouldn't have been any story to tell. I told him the whole thing.

"None of what you said surprises me," Mac said. "Especially the part about Sarge. If you've been around as long as I have, you get a pretty good handle on who can take care of themselves. Besides, he's a pretty big guy."

"You were going to tell me about him," I said.

"I'll tell you what I know and some of what I think I know and—Hey, how you doing?" Mac yelled out.

Two men were sitting on a heating grate behind a building. We were almost right on top of them but I hadn't seen them. They were hidden in the shadows and the steam that was rising out of the grate. There was an empty bottle on the ground beside them.

"You two doin' fine tonight?" Mac asked.

One of them mumbled out an answer. The other didn't respond. His eyes were open but I wasn't sure he was even aware of us standing over top of him.

"You two need a place to sleep tonight?" Mac asked. "The shelter still has space."

"No shelter," the man said. His words were slurred and thick. He was drunk or stoned or something. "We're okay … leave us alone."

"Sure, we don't want to bother you, buddy. Here," Mac said. He handed the man some cigarettes. "Thought you could use these."

"Sure … thanks … you got a light?"

"'Course I do, buddy."

Mac pulled out a package of matches and the man, hands shaking, put the cigarette in his mouth. The match flared, throwing a little halo of light. As it came close to the cigarette—close to the man's face—I could make out his features. His eyes were dull and lifeless. His skin looked discoloured, like it was yellow. Maybe that was just the light from the match. He puffed on the cigarette and the end sparked to life.

"You need a meal tomorrow, you come by The Club, okay, buddy?" Mac said.

The man mumbled an answer I couldn't understand.

"See you later."

We started off down the alley.

"If I find somebody passed out and it's below freezing, I have to try and rouse 'em. Can't leave 'em there to freeze to death."

"What if you can't wake them or they wake up and tell you to leave them alone?" I asked.

"Either way I do the same. I call the police and ask them to come and pick them up. Better to be in jail than in a coffin."

"Have you ever found anybody who was … was …"

"Dead?"

I nodded.

He nodded back. "More than once. I've seen lots of things …" He shook his head slowly. "Maybe too many things."

We walked along in silence again. I felt uneasy, uncomfortable. Part of me wanted to know what he'd seen. A bigger part didn't want to hear. I needed to change the subject.

"You were starting to tell me about Sarge."

"I don't know a lot, but I'll tell you what I know. He's been on the streets—well, at least the streets around here—for about a year and a half. Before that I don't know for sure."

"But you said he was in the army … that's why they called him Sarge."

"That's what I heard."

"But you've never asked him?"

"You don't ever ask anybody anything about his past. You wait and if somebody talks, you listen."

"So you don't really know about him."

"I know it makes sense. The way you described him handling himself in the park, the way he carries himself."

"I noticed that," I said, cutting him off. "I just can't imagine how a guy in the army ends up on the street."

"Lots of people end up on the streets. Truck drivers, factory workers, businessmen, doctors."

"There are doctors living on the streets?" That couldn't be right.

"There's everybody."

"But why would a doctor end up on the streets?"

"Lots of routes to the same place, though there usually are two things that fuel the trip. Mental illness or substance abuse, usually alcohol. You've seen both already."

"But Sarge wasn't drunk and he's not crazy."

"I think they like the term 'mentally ill' better," Mac said.

"Okay, he doesn't seem mentally ill and he wasn't drunk."

"Not the two times you saw him," Mac said.

"There must be other reasons that people are on the streets."

Mac shook his head. "Not for the people I deal with. I'm not talking about kids. They hit the streets because of physical or sexual abuse, running away from a bad home situation, drug abuse, or some, a very few, just because of the thrill of being on their own. They think it's some sort of adventure. They find out pretty soon it ain't and most go back home, especially in the bad weather. In the summer the streets are filled with kids. The first good snowfall sends them all back home."

We came up to another group of men standing around a big garbage dumpster. All four of them greeted Mac enthusiastically.

"Looks a bit like rain tonight," Mac said, looking skyward. It was overcast.

"Hope not," one of them replied.

"Well, if it does, you know what you can do, eh?"

"Get wet," another answered and they all laughed.

"That or go into a shelter. Heaton House would still have space."

"They can keep their space."

As Mac talked to them, they passed a bottle from person to person. It was offered to Mac.

"Thanks but no thanks," Mac said politely.

"How about you?" the man asked, holding the bottle out to me.

I backed away, holding my hands up, shocked. I couldn't even imagine what diseases I could get sharing anything with this bunch.

"He's too young to drink," Mac said, answering for me.

"Never too young or too old."

Mac reached into his backpack and pulled out a package of cigarettes. "You boys want to split these?"

"Thanks, Mac."

"You're a real buddy."

We started off again.

"Do you give out cigarettes to everybody?" I asked.

"Best way to gain their trust and that's the best way to help them. Nobody accepts help from somebody they don't trust."

I guess that made sense. Besides, getting cancer wasn't what was going to kill these guys.

"If those men aren't going to a shelter, where will they sleep tonight?" I asked.

"I think they were standing right beside it."

"The building?"

"The dumpster," Mac said.

"They're going to sleep in a dumpster?"

"It gets them out of the wind. They can pull down the top for protection to keep dry if it rains. Not a bad place."

"But a dumpster ... how could they sleep with all that garbage?"

"There's garbage and then there's garbage. That dumpster is used by a furniture factory. The stuff they put in there, pieces of wood, bits of leather or plastic and foam, it makes a good place to sleep."

"But why wouldn't they just go to that place you mentioned ... what was it?"

"Heaton House. It's a men's shelter. They can get a bed and a bath there."

"That doesn't sound bad. Why don't any of these guys want to go to a shelter?" I asked.

"Lots of people do use shelters, but just as many others don't."

We crossed a busy street and headed off into the dark of another back lane.

"Why wouldn't everybody go sleep in a shelter?" I asked.

"Lots of reasons. It can be crowded and loud and sometimes dangerous. There can be fights, people rippin' off your stuff. Some people can't stand being around people who're mentally ill. And some people just can't go. They're banned."

"Banned? What would somebody have to do to get banned?"

"Stealing, beating on people, or just being too crazy—"

"Don't you mean mentally ill?" I asked, chiding him.

"Nope. Crazy. Maybe being up all night screaming and yelling."

"Still, that has to be better than sleeping in a dumpster."

"There are some places that are better than both. Sometimes some of the boys get together, pool their money, and get a motel room or even a room that they can share for the winter. Sometimes they cobble together some boards and plastic and plywood and make a little shanty."

"A shanty?"

"A shack. There's a few of those down by the lake and more than a dozen under the freeway just over from here."

"And the police and the politicians let them do that?"

"As long as they stay in places where regular people don't see 'em then nobody bothers them. Others sleep under bridges, over top of sewer grates like those two guys we saw earlier, or in clothing drop boxes, doorways, telephone booths or bus shelters or—" He was counting on his fingers as he listed all the places.

"You can't be serious. You can't sleep in a telephone booth or a bus shelter," I said.

"You can sleep standing up if you're tired enough," Mac said. "Some have their own tents."

"Where would you pitch a tent?"

"Shelby Park, where you met Sarge. There's a spot in the middle where there's half a dozen tents. Come on, I'll show you."

"Should we be going there now?" I asked anxiously.

"It isn't a place *you* should ever be going by yourself, but if you're with me you're safe … well, at least pretty safe." He paused. "You want me to drop you off instead?"

"No, I'll come with you," I said reluctantly. It wasn't that I didn't trust Mac but he was old, and not that big, and his baseball bat was back at the soup kitchen.

We came out of the back alleys and onto a street. The lights and traffic were reassuring. This wasn't my world, but at least it was familiar. As we walked we passed by more people—homeless people—moving along. It was like some sort of migration … No, that wasn't right. A migration meant moving somewhere. These people were moving, but they were going nowhere.

The park was just up ahead. I felt increasingly uneasy. My anxiety increased as we entered, and my shoes crunched on the gravel path. This was certainly better than walking along the path without shoes. Would those three thugs be here in the park tonight, or would there be somebody even worse? If everybody on the street had a weapon, did Mac have one with him now? His baseball bat was a long ways away but maybe he had something else on him—a metal bar or a knife … maybe a gun. I shook my head. Yeah, right, he had a gun … maybe he had a bazooka up his sleeve.

Mac left the path and headed in through the bush. If going through the park wasn't safe, how much more dangerous was it to go off the path and into the forest? As Mac picked his way through the undergrowth, I tried to stay as close as possible. The ground was uneven and there were roots and stones sticking up. I moved as carefully as I could but in the darkness I kept stumbling and bumping into Mac.

"Do you know where you're going?" I asked.

"Does anybody really know where they're going?" he asked.

Great, just what I needed—a philosophy lesson.

"There's where we're going," Mac said. "Look."

Up ahead I caught glimmers of light flickering through the trees. It couldn't be ... it looked like—

"It's a fire."

We pushed through the last trees and found ourselves standing in a little clearing. In the opening were five tents and in the middle of the tents was a metal barrel, cut down low to the ground, holding a fire. Around the fire, sitting on lawn chairs, were eight or ten shadowy figures, their features lit up just a little by the flickering flames of the fire. This was unreal. We'd wandered out of the city, through a few trees, and into some sort of surreal campground. I half expected Yogi the bear to poke his head out of the trees and ask for a picnic basket!

"Mind if we join you gentlemen?" Mac asked.

A couple of men spun around to look in our direction. The others didn't seem to hear him.

"Come on over, always room for one or two more!" one of the men yelled out.

As we walked into the light of the campfire, I realized why the others hadn't responded. They were asleep—or more likely passed out—in their chairs.

Mac sat down on an empty stump and motioned for me to sit on the rock beside him. The fire was big enough to throw out heat and light. The warmth felt good.

The ground was littered with empty bottles. I tried to look at the bottles without being too obvious. Some of them were wine bottles—nothing fancy, and all with what appeared to be screw-top caps. There was also a bottle of cooking sherry. The other bottles had fallen label down and I couldn't tell what they were.

"Anybody seen Sarge tonight?" Mac asked.

"In there," one of the men said, gesturing to a green tent off to the side. "He turned in early."

That was why Mac had brought me here—this was where Sarge lived. I couldn't help but wonder if he'd gone to sleep or if he'd passed out like his buddies. I tried to figure out if any of these guys were at dinner tonight. It was hard to tell. In the dim, flickering light, buried underneath their toques and beards and dirt and layers of clothes they all looked pretty much the same to me. Maybe a couple of them had been at The Club tonight.

As Mac continued to talk, I felt a drop of moisture on my cheek. And then another and another. Great, it was starting to rain. A few degrees colder and snow would have been better.

"Mac … maybe we better get going—it's raining."

"We better. You guys might want to get inside too."

Seven

MAC WALKED ME to a fairly busy intersection. There were lots of cars and people … regular people—couples walking hand in hand, and groups walking along the sidewalk, going to or from restaurants or the theatre or maybe the movies or shopping. We had travelled only about five blocks but we'd left behind one world and entered another—one much more familiar to me.

Mac had offered to stay and wait with me for my ride, but I told him to go on his way. He still had to finish his rounds. I'd used my cellphone to call home and I'd spoken to Berta. My parents still weren't home and she was on her way down to get me.

I watched the cars driving by. Half of them had bluish lights. Those were the type that expensive luxury cars like Mercedes, BMWs, Audis, and a dozen other types of prestige cars all had. It was amazing how many expensive cars there were—how many people had so much money to spend. And as I stood there watching and waiting I wondered—how many of those people driving in those expensive cars passed by the parks and alleys where the homeless were sitting or shuffling or sleeping, and never knew that there was anybody outside of the climate-controlled, leather-seated, CD surround sound that encircled them? How could some people have so much and others so little?

There was a gentle beep of a horn and a silver Mercedes rolled to a stop. It was Berta driving my mother's car. At night or on long trips she'd often drive my mother's car because her own car was so old that it wasn't particularly reliable. I grabbed the door and pulled it open, jumping inside without disturbing the flow of traffic too much. It was good to get into the car and out of the rain that had started falling more heavily. Wet and near freezing temperature was a bad combination.

"Hello, Eon."

"Thanks for coming to get me," I said as I snapped on my seatbelt.

Berta pulled away.

"I'm sorry to make you come out so late. I thought my parents would be home by now."

"They got home just before I left. I offered to go because they looked … they looked … tired."

Tired. That meant they'd both probably been drinking. I doubted that it involved anything with a screw top.

"Did you have a good evening?" Berta asked.

"I don't know if 'good' is the right word." We were passing Selby Park. "You see that park there," I said, pointing to the scene rolling by outside the passenger window. "There are people who live in there."

Berta nodded but didn't answer.

"Really. I'm serious. They have tents and chairs and there's a bunch of them sitting around a fire right now."

"And how do *you* know that?" she asked.

That was stupid. I shouldn't have said anything. "Is this just between me and you?" I asked.

"If that is what you want, Eon."

I knew I could trust Berta. "I was with Mac, the man who runs the soup kitchen. I went with him on one of the walks he does every night to look out for people who are living on the streets. Mac told me there are thousands and thousands living on the streets," I explained.

Berta shook her head in disbelief. "Thousands … so hard to believe. I only see a few."

"That's what *I* said! Tonight I saw them, where they live in alleys and dumpsters and parks."

"These are not good places for you to go," Berta said. "Maybe it is better that your mother doesn't know about these things."

"I'm not telling her. She probably wouldn't believe it even if I did tell her."

"She might believe. There are homeless everywhere. That is how it is in Guatemala."

The park disappeared from view.

"I hadn't really thought about that. Are there many?"

"Many thousands."

"I didn't know that. I figured it was just like Mexico and there weren't many street people."

Berta laughed. "They do not have beggars in the fancy resorts where you and your family stayed. They are hidden like here. The same way."

"At least in Guatemala they don't have to worry about freezing to death like they do here."

"Freezing to death is not what they fear."

“What do they fear?”

Berta didn’t answer. She stared straight ahead out the windshield, the wipers moving silently across the glass to clear away the rain that had gotten even harder.

“Berta … what do they have to fear?”

She still didn’t answer right away and I thought she wasn’t going to when she started. “In my country people on the street die all the time.”

“I guess even in a warm country you can still starve to death.”

“They do not starve. They are killed. Dozens and dozens. Maybe hundreds. Maybe more. They are gunned down.”

I could scarcely believe what she was saying. “Can’t the police or the army protect them?”

“The police and army,” Berta sneered. “Who do you think does the killing?”

“That can’t be right.”

“Right it is not. True it is. I … I should not be telling of these things. Not now. Not yet.”

“Why not?”

“It is too soon.”

“I’m almost sixteen, Berta. I can handle it.”

“It is not that it is too soon for you, Eon. It is too soon for *me*.”

Eight

"IAN!"

I turned around. It was Robert. He moved around the crush of kids streaming through the corridor toward classes.

"So why weren't you there Friday night?" Robert asked.

"Why wasn't I where?" I asked.

"Jen's party."

"I forgot all about it," I said.

"You missed a good party. Lots of food, some beer, lots of ladies."

"So where were you?" Justin asked.

"Community service hours for civics."

"On a Friday night?" he asked in disbelief.

"Like I have a choice. I have to put in the hours. No hoice."

"Too bad. A couple of the girls were even asking bout you."

"Anyone in particular?" I asked.

"The usual suspects."

The bell rang, loud, echoing through the hall and etting off a wave of activity as lockers slammed and kids urried to class.

"See you at lunch," Robert said.

"Sure. See you."

I had completely forgotten about that party and I had been looking forward to it.

We filed into class. I just hoped I could get my usual seat at the back of the room.

"Ian?" Mrs. Watkins asked.

I stopped. Instinctively I wondered just what it was that I'd done wrong, or failed to read, or hadn't handed in. But really there was nothing … at least nothing that I could remember.

"So, did you go back to your placement this weekend?" she asked.

I stopped by her desk. "I was there on Friday night. put in six hours."

"In one night?" She sounded surprised or like she wa doubting me.

"It was a long night. There are lots of people to fee and lots of work to do. I'm going back tonight."

"I'm impressed."

"Impressed or surprised?" I asked.

She gave a little smirk. "Both. You think you coul tell your classmates about your placement at the end c class today?"

"I could … I guess."

"Excellent."

I turned to walk away. By now all the seats in the bac of the class were taken. I did a quick scan of the roon The only open seats were in the front row. I took the o farthest off to the side.

"Now as you recall," Mrs. Watkins began, "from our la class, we learned that, contrary to what some people m have thought, Lester Pearson was not a left winger for t

Toronto Maple Leafs. We learned that he was a Canadian prime minister who received the Nobel Prize in 1957. Does anybody remember what Nobel Prize he received?"

There was no answer. It wasn't that I didn't know, or that lots of people didn't remember, it was just that we didn't necessarily volunteer what we knew.

"Surely somebody must remember?" she prodded.

"Best supporting actor?" a voice chipped in from the back to accompanying laughter.

"How about if I give everybody an additional assignment if somebody doesn't give me the right answer," Mrs. Watkins said.

"Peace, he got it for peace!" a voice yelled out.

"Right. It's good to know that I'm not *completely* wasting my breath when I talk. This Nobel Peace Prize was awarded to Lester Pearson because of his pivotal role in the conception and creation of the United Nations Peacekeeping Force. Since 1956 there have been peacekeeping missions throughout the world. These missions have been in Europe, the Middle East, Africa, Asia, Central and South America. Does anybody know exactly what roles are played by peacekeepers?"

"Keeping the peace would be my guess, Mrs. Watkins," Kelsey said.

She shook her head slowly as the chuckling died down. "The roles of the peacekeeper can vary tremendously. Peacekeepers can be used to disarm warring factions, to protect or repatriate refugees," she said, tapping her pencil on the desk as she recited the list, ensure human rights, supervise governments or elections of governments, train or supervise local police forces, ensure the distribution of relief supplies, and most often, stand as a thin *blue* line between sides that are, or *were,* at war." She paused. "Why did I say blue line? And before anybody can give a smart-ass answer it has nothing to do with hockey."

"Because that's the colour of their helmets, berets, and vehicles," said a girl sitting just behind me.

"Obviously at least one person has done their reading," Mrs. Watkins said, trying to look stern. "Since most armed forces try to avoid being seen, their uniforms and vehicles are in browns or greens or sand colours, depending on the region where the conflict is taking place. Rather than trying to blend in, the UN peacekeepers want to be seen. By being seen it is hoped that they can avoid being mistaken as a combatant." Mrs. Watkins took a sip from the coffee sitting on her desk. "Since 1956 Canada has had over a hundred thousand members of our armed forces in these missions. We have contributed more soldiers to more missions than any other country. That is why we are known around the world as a peace-loving country."

"Obviously nobody's been watching us play hockey," somebody added.

"Obviously not," Mrs. Watkins agreed. "But there is a cost. Peacekeeping missions, although sanctioned by the United Nations, are primarily paid for by the countries that supply the soldiers. There is also another cost." She paused. "Being dressed in a blue helmet or driving in a blue vehicle doesn't make you bulletproof. Since its inception there have been over eighteen hundred deaths of United Nations peacekeepers."

There was a gasp from the class, but not from me.

knew the number because I'd done the reading on Sunday. I'd actually found it pretty interesting.

"This number seems large, but remember that there have been hundreds and hundreds of thousands of soldiers from countries around the world that have been posted in these missions. Does anybody know which country has suffered the most fatalities?"

"India," I said quietly.

"That's right, Ian," she said, spinning around to face me. I didn't think she would have heard me. "They have suffered one hundred and nine deaths. Ian, do you know which country has had the second-most deaths?"

"Canada. One hundred and seven … and counting."

She nodded. "And counting. As we speak, there are Canadians serving in missions in the former Yugoslavia, Africa and Central America, the Middle East and Asia. For a relatively small armed forces—we have approxi-
nately sixty thousand men and women in uniform—we
tretch ourselves around the globe." Mrs. Watkins took
nother sip from her coffee. "Just out of curiosity, does
nybody here have a member of their family who is in
e armed forces?"

There was no response.

"Does anybody even *know* anybody who is in the
ilitary?"

Again no answer.

"Surely *somebody* must know *somebody* who *was* in
e military."

"I do," I said. "Sort of."

"He was sort of in the military or you sort of know
m?" Mrs. Watkins asked.

"I sort of know him."

"Is this somebody you've talked to recently?"

"This past week."

"And will you be talking to him in the near future?" she asked.

"Probably … I could … I guess."

"In that case I have an assignment for you, Ian."

I cringed. Why hadn't I kept my mouth shut instead o showing off?

"Actually it's an assignment for Ian or anybody els who would like to earn some bonus marks."

"So this is a voluntary assignment?" somebody asked

"Completely," she said. "Although there are som people who could clearly use the bonus marks if the hope to make grade ten civics a one-year project."

She wasn't looking at me but I knew she was talkin to me.

"The assignment is to interview a member of th armed forces. To ask him, or her, about where they wer assigned, to discover if they were part of a Unite Nations–sanctioned peace mission, to get their opinion to hear of their experiences. That is the assignment. An questions?"

The only question I had was whether I could afford risk not doing this assignment. I didn't think that was option.

"Before we go any further discussing our reading, I like to take this opportunity to have Ian tell us about h community service placement," Mrs. Watkins said.

Great, I'd thought she'd forgotten about me. I slow got to my feet and turned around so I was facing the cla

I guess that was one good thing about sitting in the front—although if I'd been in the back, and kept my mouth shut, she probably wouldn't have remembered I was even there.

"If I'm not mistaken, Ian is the last person in the class to report on his placement. Is there anybody else?" she asked.

Nobody answered. I just stood there, on display—the poster boy for being the last. Was she trying to make me look stupid?

"Please begin, Ian."

"Sure. I'm volunteering at a place called the Club. It's a place that feeds street people."

"Do they, like, give out sandwiches or something?" a girl asked.

"No, it serves meals, real meals … beef stew and spaghetti … things like that. It's good food."

"Sounds like you've tried the food," Mrs. Watkins commented.

"I know what it looks and smells like and the people eally seem to like it," I said. I didn't want anybody to know that I'd eaten there. "I help serve the food and clean up afterwards."

"So you're like the cafeteria ladies," a guy at the back—Jason—said and then chuckled. I'd known him since grade five. I hadn't liked him since grade five.

"Do you have to wear a hairnet too?" Chris, his friend, said.

There were a couple more muffled chuckles. I crossed my arms over my chest and stared at the two guys—the two *jerks*. I looked at one and then the other and then focused on the first, locking eyes. I stared Jason down until he dropped his eyes to the desk. Jerk. Wimpy jerk. Maybe out there on the downtown streets I wasn't tough, but here was a different thing.

"People who've never been there might be tempted to make *stupid* comments," I said, my eyes still on the two guys, daring them to say something, even let a smirk cross their faces. Neither did.

"It's not just about serving food, it's about saving lives. These people would die if it wasn't for programs like this one."

"It sounds like you're really making a difference," Mrs. Watkins said.

"Not me," I protested. "I just show up and help out a little. The guy who makes it work is Mac. He lives there."

"It's not uncommon for people running these sorts of places to spend an enormous amount of hours at their work so it seems like they practically live there," Mrs. Watkins said.

"No, you don't understand ... he really *does* live there ... in the back. But it also is his life."

"It sounds like you admire what he does."

"I guess I do," I admitted, although I'd never reall thought about it until this conversation.

I had been confused by what Mac did, by his dedi cation, although I also gave him credit. Whether yo believed it was something admirable or not, you had t admit that he was prepared to back his beliefs with h actions. He walked the walk. He reminded me of Ber that way. She was always doing something for her churc or driving people to things like hospital appointments, ar

I didn't even want to guess how much money she'd sent back to support foster children in Guatemala.

"Do you think that this gentleman would be willing to come to our class and speak sometime?" Mrs. Watkins asked.

I burst out laughing before I pulled the laughter back inside. "He's pretty busy." Way too busy to waste his time talking to a bunch of kids in some stupid civics class, I thought but didn't say.

"He sounds really dedicated," Mrs. Watkins said approvingly. She turned to the class. "I was wondering, when people think of street people, what comes to mind? Give me one word, just throw them out. One word."

"Homeless," Kelsey said.

"Definitely homeless or they wouldn't be on the street. What else?"

"Drunks."

"Drug addicts," Justin said.

"Runaways."

"No," I said. "Not the people we're feeding. These aren't kids. These are men, almost all men, older men. Some are really, really old."

"Other words?" Mrs. Watkins asked.

"Bums."

"Hobos."

"Crazy as a loon," one of the two jokers at the back said.

"The term is mentally ill," I said. I wasn't finding either of them particularly funny today or any other day.

"Calling people crazy or loony, or saying they're a few bricks short of a load, or are a nut, is all part of a dangerous process," Mrs. Watkins said. "If somebody is a nut, then they are no longer a person, and if they are not a person, then you can treat them as *less*. That dehumanizing process allows people to feel it is acceptable to treat them badly." Mrs. Watkins took another sip from her coffee. "Any other words?"

"Worthless," a girl, Heather, said.

Nobody said anything. The word just hung there and everybody just stared at it. I knew this girl. She was smart and nice. She hadn't said it to be mean or a smartass.

"Ian?" Mrs. Watkins said. "Are these street people worthless?"

I shook my head slowly. "Nobody is worthless."

"I guess the real question isn't are they worthless, but are they worth *less* … less than other people."

Nobody volunteered an answer.

"Ian?"

I knew what the correct answer was, what I was expected to say—that they were worth just as much as anybody else.

"Well?"

"I'm supposed to say that everybody is worth the same," I said. "But that's not the way we treat them."

"How do we treat them?" Mrs. Watkins asked.

"We treat them like they're worth practically nothing, so maybe that's what society really does think of them," I said.

The bell rang, startling me so much that I flinched.

"On that note, class dismissed."

People started getting up and gathering their books and belongings.

"And I expect those who didn't complete the previous reading to complete it before starting on the next tw